**Skimming her
she placed her**

He sucked in a breath. His grip on her hip tightened. The thuds of his heartbeat perfectly matched the thuds of her own.

Andrés was a strictly short-term relationship man. He wouldn't want more than she could give, and all she could give him was one night. It was all she could give to herself.

This was meant to be, she realized, staring even deeper into his eyes. It had been from the start. If she'd known he was single, she would have refused point-blank to attend the party with him, would have spent the night alone in her tiny apartment unaware that he held the key to unlocking all the desires she'd kept buried so deep she'd hardly been aware they existed.

For this one night she could put those desires first, and do so with the sexiest man to roam the earth, the man who had the power to turn her to liquid without even touching her.

A man who wouldn't want anything more from her.

Michelle Smart's love affair with books started when she was a baby and would cuddle them in her cot. A voracious reader of all genres, she found her love of romance established when she stumbled across her first Harlequin book at the age of twelve. She's been reading them—and writing them—ever since. Michelle lives in Northamptonshire, England, with her husband and two young Smarties.

Books by Michelle Smart

Harlequin Presents

Claiming His Baby at the Altar
Innocent's Wedding Day with the Italian
Christmas Baby with Her Ultra-Rich Boss

A Billion-Dollar Revenge

Bound by the Italian's "I Do"

Scandalous Royal Weddings

Crowning His Kidnapped Princess
Pregnant Innocent Behind the Veil
Rules of Their Royal Wedding Night

Visit the Author Profile page
at Harlequin.com for more titles.

Michelle Smart

CINDERELLA'S ONE-NIGHT BABY

Recycling programs
for this product may
not exist in your area.

ISBN-13: 978-1-335-59230-9

Cinderella's One-Night Baby

Copyright © 2024 by Michelle Smart

Harlequin Enterprises ULC
22 Adelaide St. West, 41st Floor
Toronto, Ontario M5H 4E3, Canada
www.Harlequin.com

Printed in U.S.A.

CINDERELLA'S
ONE-NIGHT BABY

CHAPTER ONE

THE BORDERS BETWEEN the tiny principality of Monte Cleure and the countries it was sandwiched between, France and Spain, had, for generations, been lax. A wave of your passport at a bored border guard or a facial recognition scan had been considered the height of security. As the principality was considered to be Monaco on steroids and awash with millionaires and billionaires taking sanctuary in its low tax regime, this laxness, along with its notoriously lazy, corrupt police force meant it also attracted the more unscrupulous, namely drugs, arms and people traffickers who found Monte Cleure the perfect place to launder their dirty money.

This shameful attitude to law and order came to an abrupt end when its internationally loathed monarch and ruler, King Dominic, met an untimely end in a racing accident and his sister, Catalina, reluctantly took the throne. One of her first acts on being crowned Queen a couple of years before was to crack down on the criminals who used her beautiful land for their nefarious enterprises. Which meant tightening controls at the borders. Within months of Catalina taking the throne, the borders were strengthened and mandatory retraining given. Any guard suspected of corruption was sacked and new recruits taken on. One of those new recruits was Gabrielle Breton.

A year into the job and Gabrielle still loved it. It wasn't the path she'd intended to take in life, but she'd determined to make the best of it. No two days were the same. For sure, most days were routine but on days like today, when a tip-off had come in that a luxury car was being used to smuggle a million euros of cocaine into the principality from Spain, the excitement would swell inside her. She always made sure to hide it, of course. Gabrielle took pride in her professionalism, a pride that had seen her immediate supervisor recently encourage her to apply for a promotion. It was something she was still carefully considering. Gabrielle rarely did anything without careful consideration.

The main problem with the luxury car tip-off was that luxury cars accounted for roughly seventy per cent of the vehicles that passed the border. If you didn't have pots of cash there was little point in visiting. Fortunately extra information had been provided. The car in question was a brand-new model and would be driven by a man and a woman.

With barely an hour to go until her shift finished, Gabrielle and her team had thoroughly searched nine cars, X-rayed three of them to be certain, and found nothing. The other team had also come up with zilch. And so it was that when a futuristic-looking sports car that looked as if it had been driven straight out of the factory approached the border, a man behind the wheel, a woman beside him, both teams willed it to join their lanes. Gabrielle's team won, and it was her turn to take the lead on it.

Waving the driver of the gleaming machine with Spanish number plates into a bay, she waited until it had parked and then indicated to the driver to wind his window down.

A darkly handsome, black-haired man with a thick designer beard duly obliged.

'Passports, please,' she said politely in Spanish.

'I am already on your system,' the man replied with more than a hint of impatience. 'I am entitled to use facial recognition.'

She vaguely recognised him, was quite certain this was a face she'd seen when on facial recognition duty and possibly in the media too. But that made no difference to the job in hand.

'I asked for your passports.'

Strong jaw clenching, long fingers with short, buffed nails handed them over. 'Is there a problem?'

She opened the first passport. 'We shall find out shortly, Mr... Morato.' Andrés Javier Morato. Spanish national. Recently turned thirty-three.

Gabrielle glanced at his passenger before opening the second passport. Sophia Maribel Morato. Spanish national. Thirty-five. 'What is your purpose for visiting Monte Cleure?'

'What is the purpose of asking that?'

'The purpose is for my job, sir.'

Lips that could only be described as sensuous tightened in a scowl. 'I have property and business interests here. I put a *lot* of money into your economy.'

She resisted yawning. 'Congratulations. The purpose of your visit?'

'The purpose of this particular visit, *miss*...' the *miss* had a nice dismissive ring to it '...is tonight's party at the palace. I am a friend and invited guest of your Queen.'

'Lucky you.' She swore half the people crossing the border that day were attending Queen Catalina's party. Gabrielle would have happily sold one of her kidneys for an invitation to be under the same roof as the woman she idolised, but as that was as likely to happen as Gabrielle growing a second head, she kept her tone disinterested and professional. 'And if you want to address me, it's *officer*. Are you concealing any illegal drugs of any quantity on your person or in your vehicle, or any other goods that run contrary to the laws of Monte Cleure?'

He gave her the kind of look she'd expect to receive if asking whether he ate pet goldfish straight from the bowl.

'No,' he said tightly. 'I have nothing illegal in my possession or anything I need to declare. Are we done? Only, we're already running late. I have a team of people due at my apartment in twenty minutes to prepare Sophia and myself for the Queen's party.'

'I'm afraid we are not done yet, sir, and name-dropping the Queen isn't going to make the process go any faster. Please step out of the car. Both of you.'

Eyes almost as black as his hair and beard lasered with fury onto her. 'Do you know who I am?'

That old chestnut. Nearly as common and as tedious as the *I put a lot of money into your economy* one. 'I'm sure you are very important, sir, but I have a job to do and I need you to comply.'

The man's wife, who'd been silently observing, tapped his wrist with the hand her huge diamond engagement ring and thick wedding band resided on, and made a gesture with her head before pressing something on the door. It lifted up like something from a sci-fi movie.

With a put-upon sigh, Andrés followed suit, unfolding what turned out to be an incredibly tall, muscular body from the car. His wife was much smaller, only a few inches taller than Gabrielle, although the heels she wore made her appear statuesque.

'Stand behind the line, please.' Gabrielle pointed where she needed them to go, just a couple of feet from the bay the car was parked in. Sophia didn't need telling twice. Andrés though, folded his arms across his broad chest, pecs flexing beneath the black shirt. The sleeves were rolled to the elbows, revealing a sleeve tattoo on his left arm that, at first glance, looked surprisingly tasteful.

'Why?'

'We need to search your car and regulations don't allow us to do that until you're behind the line.' She indicated her two colleagues and the sniffer dog waiting patiently for the go ahead.

Varying forms of anger and outrage contorted the handsome face. 'How long is this going to take?'

'It will take as long as it takes.'

'I need you to fast track it.'

'I'm afraid your friend the Queen dislikes it when we cut corners. Now stand behind the line, *sir.*'

For a moment she thought it quite possible that his head would explode.

A year ago, Gabrielle would have found it intimidating having a man twice her size staring down at her with such arrogant loathing. She could practically read what he was thinking: *No one told Andrés Morato what to do! Car searches were for the hoi polloi, not for someone as important as him!*

'It's your own time you're wasting,' she helpfully reminded him.

Nostrils on the patrician nose flared. Chiselled jaw clenched hard enough to grind wheat. And then he saw sense, walking backwards three steps without removing his 'I'm going to make you pay for this inconvenience' gaze from her.

'Thank you for your co-operation, sir.'

'If you damage it in any way, officer, you will pay for the repairs.'

'Don't worry, sir, the money you put into my country's economy means we can afford it.'

Andrés stared at the diminutive woman politely bossing him around and politely using his words as weapons back at him, and the fury that had been curdling his stomach all week grew. 'What are you hoping to find?'

Her response was to squeeze her hands into

latex gloves and pretend not to hear him. But she had heard, of that he was certain.

Andrés was not used to being ignored. He was not used to being bossed around. He was used to deferment. His family was the only exception to this, and it was only because of his sister that he'd dragged himself out of bed that morning instead of catching up on all the sleep he'd missed in recent weeks thanks to the legal letter that had rocked the foundations of his world. The last thing he wanted was to socialise with hundreds of people.

His good friend and business partner on a number of ventures, the king consort, would have understood if he'd cancelled. Sophia would have sulked until Christmas. This was a day she'd been hugely looking forward to, and so, Andrés had done his best to keep his bad mood to himself. He thought he'd been successful, right until his helicopter landed in Barcelona and he'd got behind the wheel of his brand-new toy.

Sophia had put her seatbelt on and faced him. 'We don't have to go to the party if you don't want.'

He'd glared at her. 'You could have said that before we left Seville.'

'I was hoping you'd cheer up. I haven't seen

you in a month. The least you can do is pretend to be happy at spending time with me.'

He'd put the car into gear without another word and had ignored her every effort at conversation since. That the traffic had been heavy, stopping and starting at will and refusing to part like the Red Sea at his command had only added to the foulness of his mood. The hope that actually getting behind the wheel would lift his mood had been a false one. Should have taken the helicopter all the way into Monte Cleure. He'd be already in his apartment brooding that he'd have to leave it shortly and fake gregariousness for the evening, not having to deal with a jobsworth border guard.

In his best sarcastic voice, he addressed the border guard again. 'You must be searching for something, so what is it? Drugs? Counterfeit handbags? A litter of puppies?'

'If I find puppies, sir, then I will personally use this on you.' She patted the bulge at her hip, the expression on her face making it impossible to tell if she was joking or not.

'Is that a gun or a taser?' Sophia asked, finally joining in.

'A taser.'

'Can I use it on him?'

'If it was at my discretion then gladly, but I'm afraid it's against regulations and more than my job's worth, miss.' She crouched down and ran her hands beneath the wheel arch. She was so short she didn't have to crouch very far.

'That's a shame,' Sophia mused.

The guard, or *officer* as she preferred to be addressed, still examining the wheel arch, said over her shoulder to Sophia, 'I believe if you search the dark web, you can purchase your own. If in doubt about how to use it, just aim and press.'

Sophia laughed. 'I will certainly keep that in mind for the next time he embarrasses me by throwing his weight around.'

The officer's face didn't even flicker. 'I couldn't possibly comment.'

Andrés looked between the two women and the darkness eating at him flickered.

He was being gratuitously rude, he realised. He'd spent the day letting his sister take the brunt of his foul mood and now he was throwing his weight around with a border guard and behaving like a self-entitled brat. As bureaucratic as the officer was being, she was only doing her job.

Inhaling deeply, he held his hands up and attempted a facial expression that wasn't a glare. 'Okay, okay, I get it, I'm behaving like an ass who deserves to be tasered.'

The officer, who'd moved onto the next wheel

arch, almost smiled. Her lips, Andrés observed, were only a touch away from being too big for the rest of her face. If they weren't set a normal distance beneath her rather squashed nose he would assume she'd had them enhanced like so many women liked to do in this day and age.

Hers was an interesting face. Even more interesting; not a scrap of makeup on it. A smear of oil down the right cheekbone though. Slightly frizzy dark brown hair scraped into the kind of ponytail he hadn't seen on a female since his childhood. Absolutely no way to tell what was hidden beneath the severe, masculine uniform of dark blue shirt and trousers and polished black steel-capped boots.

His phone vibrated in his pocket. It was his lawyer. This was the call he'd been waiting for, the call that could either shift the darkness or push him further into it.

Forgetting all about the pocket-sized officer's interesting face and nondescript body, he moved away from Sophia to answer it.

Although Gabrielle was in no way intimidated by the man, she found herself breathing a little easier when Andrés turned his back and walked away to take his call. He wasn't intimidating but *unnerving*, she decided.

His wife though, was the complete opposite, and quickly struck up conversation. In no time at all, she was telling Gabrielle all about the boutique she owned and designed the clothing for, which explained the gorgeous floaty dress she was wearing, and how she didn't particularly like leaving Seville but when it came to a party with royalty then who was she to refuse?

It was rare that someone whose ultra-expensive car was being subjected to a forced search was friendly and chatty. Usually they behaved like Sophia's husband and sulked like small children. Gabrielle was an expert on small children. Even when face down on the floor having a temper tantrum because you had the temerity to say no to them, they were easier to deal with than entitled billionaires of either sex. One thing life had taught Gabrielle, long before she'd become a border guard, was that rich people were a law to themselves. This billionaire, Sophia Morato, was a refreshing change, even if she did make Gabrielle feel like a moon eclipsed by the sun. It wasn't just her slender beauty, but her vivaciousness and the ease she so clearly felt in her own skin. It was an ease Gabrielle envied. In truth, it would be easy to envy everything about Sophia Morato...with the exception of her arrogant husband. Imagine having to deal with that rude, entitled attitude every day. Having the looks and physique of a Greek god in no way mitigated that.

He really was gorgeous though, and as he pocketed his phone and walked back to his wife, Gabrielle had to stop her eyes from wandering to him for another gawp and concentrate on her search of the car's bonnet. Not only was gawping unprofessional but he was a married man.

'How are you getting on?' he asked Gabrielle in a much lighter tone than he'd used before.

'So far, so good.'

'Do you think it will take much longer?' No sign of impatience. Whatever his conversation had been about, it had definitely had a positive effect on him. Maybe he'd lost a billion euros and just learned it had been found down the back of a sofa. Gabrielle had lost ten Monte Cleure dollars recently and had cheered right up when she found it in the back pocket of her jeans.

'Depends if we find anything.' The longer the search had gone on, the more inclined she'd been to call the whole thing off and send the Moratos on their way. She would bet her salary they had nothing illegal stashed in it. Gizmo, the sniffer dog, hadn't reacted at all. But she had a job to do, a job where cutting corners was forbidden, and the search would be completed with the thoroughness demanded.

Bonnet done with, Gabrielle opened the tiny boot. It contained a mandatory breakdown kit and nothing else. Gizmo had a good sniff but, again, nothing.

Suppressing a sigh, she carefully lifted the boot's luxury floor carpet and opened the hatch beneath it. With practised ease, she removed the spare tyre.

'They get the smallest person on the team to do the heavy lifting?'

She flicked her gaze to the Spaniard. His arms were folded loosely across his chest, a half-smile on his face and a thick black eyebrow raised.

'I'm fitter than I look.'

'So I see.'

Although he was only making an observation, something fluttered deep in the pit of Gabrielle's stomach.

'Do you work out?'

'Only if you count lifting spare tyres as working out—being a single mother and holding down a job doesn't leave much time for gym memberships.'

She had no idea why she'd just mentioned being a mother.

Sophia did an exaggerated double-take. 'You have a child? How old?'

Although Gabrielle knew there was little danger in talking about Lucas, especially with people whose paths she would never cross outside this border, her stomach still tightened. Time had only eased the terror that had cloaked her in the days and weeks and months after bringing Lucas home, not eradicated it completely.

'Four,' she answered with practised steadiness.

'You must have been young.'

'Nineteen.'

'And you're a single mother?'

'It's just me and Lucas.' And that's exactly how it had to stay. It was far too dangerous for Gabrielle to entertain anything else.

'That must be tough.'

She could have no idea. 'Sometimes.'

'Do you get much help?'

'My mother helps as much as she can—Lucas is spending the weekend with her and my brother, which is great for all of them.' Even if it meant Gabrielle returning to her apartment and physically hurting at Lucas's absence.

Closing the boot lid, she patted it gently. 'We're all done here.'

Gizmo hadn't reacted to the spare tyre. The car was clean.

'We can go?' Andrés asked.

'Once you've inspected your vehicle for any damage we might have accidentally caused and signed the form for it.'

He immediately crossed the yellow line to join her and looked at his watch.

Unable to resist, she adopted an innocent voice and said, 'Do you have to be somewhere, sir?'

Andrés snapped his attention back to the officer. It was the barely suppressed humour flitting across the interesting face that had been mostly deadpan throughout the ordeal she'd put him through that brought a short burst of laughter from his mouth. Raising an eyebrow, he said with mock seriousness, 'I don't know if you're aware but we are expected at the palace for the Queen's birthday party.'

Dark brown eyes widened in mock surprise. 'You should have mentioned it.' Then, pillowy lips tugging at the corners, she indicated the stone building that housed the Monte Cleure border staff's administrative offices. 'I'll make it as quick as I can for you. I'll start on the form. If you find damage, take a photo of it. If there isn't any, all I'll need is your signature and... Are you okay, miss?'

It took Andrés a beat to realise she'd turned her focus to Sophia. Following her gaze he saw she'd covered her hand with her mouth.

'Feel sick,' she mumbled, doubling over. 'Bathroom?'

The officer sprang into action and hurried her off into the administrative office. Andrés watched them disappear inside, perplexed that his sister, who'd been perfectly normal up to that point had, without any warning or build-up or hints that anything was wrong, suddenly declared a need to vomit.

Not having the strongest of stomachs when it came to illness, Andrés decided to leave the officer to deal with her, and inspect his car. After close examination, he headed inside and found the officer at a desk behind a computer.

'No damage,' he confirmed. 'How's Sophia?'

She looked up at him and grimaced. 'I've given her some water but she didn't want me to stay in the bathroom…' Her words tailed off as Sophia came in through an internal door and flopped onto a visitor chair.

Running the back of a hand dramatically over her forehead, she said, 'Andrés, I feel awful. I don't think I can make it to the party.'

He stared at her with narrowed eyes. His sister had always been a terrible actress and this over-the-top performance reminded him of when she would try to convince their mother she was too ill for school.

'I was sick twice,' she insisted into the silence, then lowered her voice and weakened it to add, 'Can you imagine if I gave the Queen an illness? On her birthday?'

He could laugh at the irony. All day he'd been like a bear with a sore head wishing to be hit by a meteor to get out of having to attend the damned party, but since receiving the excellent news from his lawyer, his mood had done a one-eighty. Now, just as he was looking forward to a night of celebrating his life not being upended after all and partying without any press intrusion, his plus one was bailing on him.

Andrés continued studying Sophia. She didn't look ill. Not in the slightest. But, he reminded himself, this was a party she'd almost cried when he asked if she wanted to go with him, a party she'd spent two months designing and creating a dress to wear for. Why would she pretend illness for something she'd been so excited about?

With a twinge of guilt for assuming she was faking, he said, 'I'll get Rich to collect us.' Rich was his helicopter pilot. The building of his Monte Cleure apartment had its own helipad. If he'd got Rich to fly them straight here all this hassle would have been avoided.

'Oh, you must go still.'

He raised both eyebrows at this uncharacteristic selflessness.

'We've travelled all this way,' she insisted. 'And it would be rude for you to cancel at such short notice. This is the Queen of Monte Cleure we're talking about. Her husband's one of your business partners.'

'If you don't come then I will be the only

person without a plus one,' he pointed out. 'The meet-and-greet part starts in two hours. The women I know who could take your place would never make it in time.' Well, there were some women who could make it, but they were women who would assume his invitation was just a short step to a marriage proposal.

Sophia's gaze drifted to the officer who'd been quietly completing the form for them to sign. Andrés followed her gaze then looked back to his sister, his brow creasing in a silent question that was answered with a subtle nod. He looked again at the officer and tried to imagine her in a ball gown. His imagination completely failed him but…

There was real merit to Sophia's silently delivered suggestion. *Real* merit.

Gabrielle had been following the conversation in the same way she followed Lucas's inane chatter when he was describing in exact detail the plot of his favourite cartoon: with one ear. It was only as she was printing off the form that would let the Moratos leave and signalled the end of her work shift that the silence suddenly became loaded.

She looked from one Morato to the other. Both were sizing her up as if she were a prize cow about to be sold off to market.

Comprehension dawned. Her mouth fell open. 'You cannot be serious?'

CHAPTER TWO

IT TURNED OUT the Moratos were completely serious. They wanted Gabrielle to take Sophia's place as Andrés's guest for the Queen's birthday party. The same Queen Gabrielle positively *idolised*. The same Queen she'd lined the streets to see, with Lucas in his buggy, and cheered for when she'd passed them in her coronation procession. The same Queen who'd enacted laws that had made Gabrielle feel a little safer.

Visions of princesses in fairy-tale dresses dancing with handsome princes in swallow-tail suits floated in her mind, of delicious food, champagne and…

'I can't go,' she said, shaking off the longing and bringing herself back down to earth. 'I don't know you and I have nothing to wear.'

'You can wear my dress,' Sophia said.

When Gabrielle realised she wasn't joking, she burst out laughing. 'You're taller and skinnier than me!'

'Not by much. There's a team at the apartment waiting to turn me into a princess for the night and make any last-minute alterations to my dress.' Her eyes narrowed as she studied Gabrielle's physique. 'The hem will obviously have to be adjusted and a little work needed around the bust and hips but it's doable in the timeframe.'

Cheeks burning at the scrutiny, she wailed, 'I can't!'

Sophia arched a brow. 'Do you have a better offer for the evening? Your son is with your mother, your work shift is over…what better way to spend a Saturday night than at the party of the decade?'

Gabrielle was fighting hard not to give hope and excitement air. It had been well over four years since she'd been on a proper night out.

The circumstances around Lucas's conception had compelled her to distance herself from her friends. By the time he was born she'd managed to alienate all of them with her refusal to discuss the father and absolute refusal to include them in anything to do with the pregnancy or birth. She still felt terrible about it, terrible for hurting the tight-knit group she'd grown up with, but she'd had no choice. The risks had been too great.

Since she'd brought Lucas home, one evening had been much the same as the next. Saturday evenings had ceased to have any meaning. Tonight, with Lucas at her brother's, Gabrielle's grand plan had involved a long bath and an action movie too old for Lucas to watch. There was no spare cash for her to go out and party even if she had friends left to party with.

'You don't even know my name,' she felt compelled to remind them *and* herself, because this whole idea was bonkers, and that they were taking it seriously only proved the Moratos themselves were bonkers and she shouldn't even be entertaining the idea, no matter how her heart soared at the thought of it.

Andrés, who'd been a silent observer propped against the wall up to this point, stretched his neck. 'What *is* your name?'

'Gabrielle. And I only know your name because the two of you and your car matched the profile of a pair of drug smugglers.'

The hint of a smile played on his lips. 'Gabrielle, if you attend the party with me, you will be sparing me from social humiliation and saving the palace staff an enormous headache—by now, the tables for the banquet will have been laid and the places set—'

'But I don't *know* you,' she interrupted. 'I can't go off with a stranger even if it is to the palace! For all I know, you two are the Spanish Bonnie and Clyde and planning to lure me to my death… No offence,' she hastened to add when she realised she'd just accused them of being notorious criminals.

The hint of a smile widened. 'None taken.

You are right to be cautious.' In two easy strides he was resting a butt cheek on her desk and leaning across to look her in the eye. 'Gabrielle, I can assure you of your safety. There is a team of people waiting to transform Sophia into a princess at my apartment—they can transform *you* into that princess. My driver will take us there and when the party has finished, deliver you to your home. You will not have to spend any time alone with me. We will be chaperoned at all times.'

Oh, but she was torn. Situations like this only happened in the movies, and it would be much easier to think logically if her airwaves hadn't suddenly become deluged with the delicious scent she'd caught a trace of when Andrés first entered the office. Not only did the man have the face and physique of a Greek God but smelt much as she imagined one would too. Some people really did have everything, and as she gazed into his black eyes, the image of the dancing princesses and handsome princes floated back into her mind and longing refilled her soaring heart. Gabrielle hadn't even attended her own senior school graduation; had missed out on all the glitz and glamour and excitement because her sister had been in no state to be left alone.

Eloise had been broken by a man whose life

was every bit as glamorous and as self-centred as Andrés Morato's.

'Andrés is a gentleman. I trust him to take care of you and to make your experience at the Queen's party one to remember for the rest of your life,' Sophia said gently, and it was with a burn of embarrassment that Gabrielle realised she'd briefly tuned out that she was in the room too. Sophia must be one trusting woman to encourage her husband to take another woman to a party as his plus one...

It suddenly became clear why they were asking this of her.

Sophia didn't have to worry about her husband making a move on plain old Gabrielle Breton and Andrés didn't have to worry about temptation. Eloise was the beauty of the Breton family. Gabrielle wasn't attractive enough to be a threat to the Moratos' marriage.

'Think of the story you will have to tell your son when he's older,' Andrés coaxed. 'The story of the night his mother went to the Queen's birthday party and dined and danced with royalty like a princess.'

Even more longing swelled in her chest. The minute Fran, her old best friend from school had turned eighteen, she'd bagged herself a part-time job amongst the palace's waiting staff and had regaled their old gang with tales of the fanciest food imaginable and a palace more spectacular than the public could imagine.

To actually attend one of those parties as a guest...

Striving to keep her professional face in place, she looked into Andrés's black eyes, so hypnotic that even if he wasn't married she'd be having to fight to stop herself from falling into them. 'If I agree...'

He nodded encouragingly, smugness already spreading over his handsome face at what would have been, to his mind, a foregone conclusion.

'*If* I agree then which Andrés Morato will I be accompanying? The spoilt brat or the less spoilt brat? Because if it's the spoilt brat I think I'll give it a miss.'

The smugness evaporated. His expression could only be described as gobsmacked.

The moment Gabrielle agreed to the outrageous suggestion, things moved terrifyingly fast. Refusing the Moratos' offer to drive her to their apartment—not only was it quicker for her to cycle but the back seat of their car was so cramped that even little old her would struggle to fit in it—she allowed herself to be talked into going straight to their apartment rather than returning to her own for essentials. Everything she needed, they assured her, would be provided.

A ten-minute bike ride later, during which she called her mother to check in on Lucas and fill her in on everything, and Gabrielle looked at the huge gold doors of the Imperium, one of Monte Cleure's most magnificent apartment blocks, and shook her head in wonder. She'd cycled past this building twice a day, four days a week for the last year, passed it numerous times in the twenty-two years before that, and never had it crossed her mind that one day she would be invited inside.

A man in a professional suit appeared like an apparition. 'Ms Breton?'

She nodded. No point asking how he knew. Her uniform was a dead giveaway. At least this meant Andrés hadn't changed his mind. It had been patently obvious from his shocked reaction to her calling him a spoilt brat that no one had called him anything insulting in a long, long time, and though he'd broken the stunned silence with laughter, she'd wondered if she'd arrive at his apartment and be given a curt note and a banning order forbidding her from entering the building.

'I'm Bernard, the Imperium's concierge. Allow Pierre to take your bicycle. I will show you to Mr Morato's apartment. He arrived three minutes ago.'

She assumed Pierre was the gangly teenager standing behind him. 'Thank you… Where will you put my bike?'

'It will be kept in storage until you or Mr Morato request it.'

'You will look after it, won't you?' she asked the teenager anxiously. She couldn't afford a replacement.

After assurances were made, Gabrielle was swept into a gorgeous atrium that reminded her of the seven-star hotel casino she'd briefly worked weekends at as a croupier when she turned eighteen. Her border guard uniform made her feel decidedly unsophisticated and out of place, and she self-consciously smoothed the strands of hair that had come loose from her ponytail and tried not to tread so heavily in her clumpy boots. Not that her own clothes would make her feel any less frumpy and out of place.

Led into a mirrored elevator with sink-your-toes-in maroon carpet and an armchair for the lazy, and which had two non-emergency buttons: up and down, Bernard doffed his hat again as the door closed on her. A short, silent ride later and the door slid open into a small room with marble floors, a small marble desk and one door. Next to the door was a security box.

It was while she was peering at the box wondering which button she needed to press that the door opened.

Andrés, shirt buttons undone revealing a muscular chest with a healthy smattering of black hair covering it, greeted her with a dazzling smile that revealed dazzlingly white, straight teeth and an outstretched hand. 'I was afraid you might have changed your mind. Forgive my state of undress but my tailor is about to make last-minute adjustments to my tuxedo.'

Not knowing where to put her eyes, aware of heated colour staining her cheeks, it took a beat longer than was polite to realise she was supposed to shake the outstretched hand. Painfully aware her own hands were filthy with oil and grime, the need for speed meaning she'd bypassed her usual end-of-shift hand-wash, Gabrielle gave it the quickest, lightest shake she could get away with. Except Andrés had other ideas, firmly wrapping his fingers around it and clasping his other hand to it, flooding skin that hadn't been cold with tingling warmth. His hands were so big compared to hers that it was like being engulfed by an oversized bear. 'Thank you for agreeing to this. I am in your debt.'

Releasing her hand with the same nonchalance with which he'd clasped it, he stepped to one side and waved a hand for her to enter. 'Please, come in.'

Absently rubbing her still-tingling hand, Gabrielle entered an apartment that made her feel so insignificant and self-conscious that if the door hadn't closed behind her, she'd have bolted.

She'd been born in Monte Cleure. The district she'd been raised in and still lived in was a tiny dot in the landscape, an anomaly compared to the grandeur the rest of their citizens lived in. Her district was protected from the bulldozers for redevelopment only because it provided the staff who worked on the yachts, in the hotels, in the penthouses, in the palace, kept law and order, and nursed people when they were sick. She'd spent her whole life in the principality she called home and she had never, until this moment, entered the home of someone outside her own district.

Too busy gawping at the gorgeous living space she'd been ushered into that in itself was twice the size of her whole apartment, taking in the multiple high sash windows, the luxurious furnishings and exquisite modern art works, she failed to notice Sophia until she was right in front of her. 'Let me introduce you to your team,' she said, taking Gabrielle's hand.

'One minute,' Andrés interrupted. 'The NDA needs to be signed first.'

That would be the non-disclosure agreement briefly discussed as they left the border force office. And *discussed* was a loose term for Andrés calling out as he strode to his car that he'd have one drawn up and ready for her to sign when she arrived at his apartment.

A pencil-thin man in a business suit appeared, seemingly from nowhere, and handed her a tablet. 'Input your details, then read the contents and sign.'

'I need to get on. Any problems, Gino can handle it,' Andrés said before disappearing through an archway.

More than a little dazed, Gabrielle did as Gino, who she assumed was Andrés's lawyer, instructed. Her details inputted, the agreement itself appeared on the screen. The language used was clear enough. Signing meant she promised not to disclose any personal details about Andrés, his home or any conversation she was privy to with him and any guest at the party, including any conversations overheard. Compared to the NDA Eloise had been tricked into signing, it wasn't particularly onerous and didn't forbid Gabrielle from talking about the party itself. Also, the reasons for signing it were completely different to Eloise's situation, so she swallowed her misgivings and signed the box indicated with her finger.

No sooner had she passed the tablet back to the lawyer than Sophia snatched hold of Gabrielle's hand and dragged her off through the same tall, wide arch Andrés had vanished through. It led into a small corridor with three doors. She opened the furthest one, plunging Gabrielle into the most stunning bedroom she'd ever seen. More than a bedroom. More like the suites found in Monte Cleure's finest hotels used exclusively by their wealthiest guests, but with a real feminine tone to it. The huge sleigh bed only took a fraction of the space. Waiting for her were five ultra-stylish women.

'Ladies,' said Sophia, 'meet Gabrielle. I need you to work your magic on her.'

For a good minute, the five women did nothing but stare critically at her. And then they swooped.

First she was ushered into an ultra-modern bathroom with a walk-in shower you could party in.

'Shampoo your hair and then use this,' the tallest of the women said, pressing a small tube into her hand. 'Keep it in for two minutes before rinsing. When you're showered, wrap your wet hair in a towel for no longer than thirty seconds. Time is of the essence—be finished in ten minutes. Make sure to use the nail brush.'

Showering orders given, the women left the bathroom.

Gabrielle stripped her uniform off and stepped under the square shower head that gave the illusion of floating off the ceiling. It was so large it could comfortably shower water on two people, and as she made that observation, an image floated in her head of Andrés standing beneath the spray, the chest she'd had that glimpse of completely bare…

Flustered at the unwanted image, flustered too at the hot, sticky feeling in the base of her abdomen, she quickly turned her attention to the digital screen inbuilt into the tiles that had an array of symbols and temperature readings on it. Not having the faintest idea what she was doing, she tentatively pressed the largest symbol, a circle, on the top left corner. In less than a second, water set at the perfect temperature cascaded over her.

Resolutely *not* thinking of the married Andrés or his naked chest, she popped the shampoo lid. It had the most delicious scent she'd ever smelt and felt like silk on her hands. If she didn't have *time is of the essence* playing on a loop in her head, she'd have washed it twice just for the pleasure. Instead she moved onto the tube, which turned out to be an anti-frizz deep conditioner. Normally only able to afford the cheapest conditioner, she happily coated her hair with it, and then, while waiting for it to do its thing, sniffed the four varieties of decidedly feminine shower gels. The first was so delicious, reminding her of lilies in bloom, that she came close to swooning. She scrubbed every inch of her body with it.

Hair and body clean and rinsed, she reluctantly pressed the circle symbol again and the cascade stopped.

Oh, well, she told herself as she wrapped the warmest, biggest, fluffiest towel around her body, at least she had a story to share with Lucas; the day mama had a taster of how the elitist of society's elite lived.

Teeth brushed, oversized fluffy robe on, she stepped back into the bedroom and found it transformed into something that resembled a beauty parlour, the dressing table chair pulled back, hair styling products and a vast array of makeup and brushes lined up and ready for use.

Sophia, sitting on the corner sofa talking to a woman with a tape measure in hand, turned her face to Gabrielle with a smile and, for that brief moment, Gabrielle found herself ashamed to meet Sophia's eye; ashamed because if she could peer into Gabrielle's mind she'd find in it that brief fantasy of Sophia's husband naked.

At least it had been unbidden and she'd cut the imagery off practically the moment it formed, Gabrielle tried to comfort herself. Tried. Because unbidden or not, it had been *her* brain that conjured the image, and though she'd steadfastly refused to allow it to form again, it made her feel terrible to know she'd betrayed this nice woman with her imagination. As far as Gabrielle was concerned, the moment a couple committed themselves, that made them off-limits, even in the mind. Marriage made that commitment sacred. Or it should.

Before Lucas, marriage was something she'd assumed would be in her future. Meet a nice man, fall in love and settle down. But the commitment of marriage meant two becoming one, a unity of complete openness and the baring of souls. For Lucas's sake, she could not risk opening her soul to anyone. The consequences of it all going wrong—and many marriages *did* go wrong—were too great.

Returning Sophia's smile, the shame in Gabrielle's chest lifted.

It had been a mental blip, that was all. When they got to the palace, it would be Queen Catalina, and the party itself that would take all her attention, not the man she was accompanying as a favour.

Andrés was sprawled on a sofa sipping bourbon, flicking through the television channels and telling himself that checking his watch every twenty seconds wouldn't make the stylists working on Gabrielle work any quicker. They had a lot of work to do with her. That wasn't a criticism, just an observation. Andrés and Sophia hadn't been born into money. He remembered well the life they'd had before weekly manicures and pedicures and thrice weekly trims became routine. That life had been one of scrimping and saving. He remembered walking to school in shoes too tight around the toes and seeing flash cars zoom by and thinking, *One day I'll drive a car like that*. He would see men in tailored suits made of the finest material and think, *One day I'll wear clothes like that*. And he would see his father return home after a long day at work to a wife who worked equally long hours, the pair of them barely able to conceal their contempt of the other, and think, *There will never come a day that I marry*. By the age of thirteen, he'd been firm in his mind about this. When he grew up, he would be rich and happy and travel the world wearing the best clothes and live exactly as he pleased, single for ever. Which meant no children. His parents were proof that children were a tie you could not escape. Children with someone you detested was a recipe for a lifetime of misery and to Andrés's mind, life was too short to spend it being miserable. If his parents wanted to spend the rest of their lives stuck together, even though their children had both long flown the family nest and the wealth Andrés shared freely with them meant they had the means to escape each other and forge new lives apart, then that was their business.

His last-minute date for the evening had the right idea. He'd seen the tightening of her mouth when Sophia had asked about her son, and guessed the relationship with the son's father had broken down and she'd sensibly decided to live apart from him. Better than making her child live in a war zone? He didn't know. His parents' marriage had been very much a verbal war zone but as a child, he'd been terrified of them splitting up. Divorce had loomed large in his mind from the day he'd first learned what it meant.

The good thing now was that the whole mess with his ex, Susi, was over. These were things he need never worry about again, and he made a mental note to call his doctor first thing and get a vasectomy arranged. It was time. He would not put himself through that again. He'd known in his heart that her child couldn't be his—he was far too careful of accidents to let that happen—but still there had been that cold spark of fear that an accident *had* happened. If the tests had proved the child to be his then he would have felt obliged to tie his life to a woman who had more sides than a hexagon.

He wondered why the father of Gabrielle's child wasn't on the scene before dismissing the thought as none of his business. She'd been very young to have a child in this day and age though. Again, not a criticism, just an observation. Andrés did not appreciate people casting judgement on his life and so made sure not to cast judgement on theirs. Her judgement on him, calling him a spoilt brat, had been deserved. His bad mood had led to him behaving atrociously, but what had shocked him had been Gabrielle's willingness to call him out on it. Only Sophia ever did that, and that was only because she was his big sister and thought it her duty.

He poured himself another bourbon—just a small one—and allowed himself a look at the time. They needed to leave in four minutes if they were going to make it to the palace before the banquet started. He'd accepted that they would miss the initial champagne reception meet-and-greet but so long as they were there in time to take their designated seats then all would...

Voices sounded, breaking through his thoughts. The team had finished with his last-minute date.

Tipping his bourbon down his throat, he rose to his feet at the same moment the most ravishing woman he'd ever set eyes on appeared through the archway.

CHAPTER THREE

GABRIELLE KNEW THE shoes Sophia had coaxed her into wearing were perfect for the dress, mainly because the heels meant they didn't need to take much of the hem up. The problem was, she hadn't worn heels since those horrid casino days, and trying to walk in them with anything like elegance was a battle she feared she would lose, and so it was that she joined Andrés in the living area of his magnificent apartment with Sophia walking behind her softly chanting, 'One foot in front of the other, one foot in front of the other,' and mentally praying not to fall flat on her face. So intense was her concentration that at first the figure rising from the far sofa was nothing but a blur in her vision. It wasn't until her heart made a powerful thump that her eyes focused.

She actually felt her lungs close up and push the air out.

It took a long beat for Andrés to recognise the ravishing woman who'd appeared under the archway with Sophia as the oil-stained bossy border guard of the unflattering uniform and masculine boots. An even longer beat for him to close his mouth.

It was Sophia who broke the silence. 'Well?'

she demanded, pointing her finger at Gabrielle. 'What do you think?'

Her words brought Andrés round from his temporary paralysis. 'I think,' he said drily, focusing on Sophia as he strode over to them, 'that you look and sound very well for someone with a sickness bug.'

'I'm feeling much better,' she said cheerfully. 'Too late to change the arrangements back to what they were though. Now tell us what you think of Gabrielle's transformation. Doesn't she look divine?'

He found he had to snatch a breath before letting his gaze fall back on his last-minute date.

It must be the starkness in the difference between the woman who had disappeared to be made over and the woman who'd returned that had caused his paralysis, he figured. The contrast was astounding. The woman standing in front of him, blushing beautifully under the weight of his scrutiny, was wearing an elegant deep blue velvet dress that swept over one shoulder and beneath the other. Flaring gracefully at the hips, it pooled in a small train behind her. Her hair was loose; thicker, glossier and longer than he'd envisaged and fell like waves down to the swell of her breasts. He would never have guessed the utilitarian uniform concealed a perfect curvy body, or guessed that a shimmer of makeup could make an interesting face come alive and turn into something beautiful.

The only thing missing was jewellery. She wore not a scrap of it. About to suggest Sophia lend her some of her own, he looked even closer and realised Gabrielle didn't need jewellery after all. She sparkled perfectly without it.

'The team have done an amazing job,' he agreed. He'd known the team he'd brought in for Sophia could make anyone look a million dollars but this was incredible. He would have to pay them a bonus. 'No one would guess from looking at her that she works as a border guard.'

'Excuse me,' the woman in question said archly, 'but I am here, you know.'

Sophia was immediately contrite. 'I'm sorry, Gabrielle. I'm just incredibly excited for you.'

The pillowy lips covered in a sheen of red lipstick tugged into a smile. 'Apology accepted.' Then dark brown eyes accentuated by subtle, smoky makeup, locked onto his. 'As for you, Mr Morato, please remember that I am a human being and treat me as such.'

If she hadn't delivered her warning—and it was a warning—with a dry wryness, he would have taken offence at the implication that he would treat her as less than human if not reminded.

He'd have taken offence when the truth was

Gabrielle was right, just as she'd been right to call him out earlier as a spoilt brat. She was setting her stall out early on how she expected to be treated and he could only respect her for it, respect her honesty; an honesty missing from the yes-men and -women he surrounded himself with. He'd been thinking about that when getting ready that evening and the tailor he'd used since he'd first earned enough to buy a fitted suit had been his usual deferential self. Because he hadn't always been deferential. When Andrés had first stepped into his tailor's shop over a decade ago, he'd been treated with politeness but there had been no reverence. That had only come about as his wealth and power had increased. It had happened in tiny increments, and not just with his tailor but everyone, staff, friends, acquaintances and lovers. They'd become nodding dogs only saying what they thought he wanted to hear.

Staring down into eyes that stared back with actual challenge and which grew more stunning the more he looked, he gave a half smile. 'Any more instructions before we leave, Miss Breton? Or is it enough that I promise not to act like a spoilt brat and promise to treat you as a human?'

Her cheeks sucked in as if she were suppressing laughter. 'A promise to give me a crash course in palace etiquette on the drive there would be helpful.'

Sophia waved them off.

After seeing Gabrielle into the limousine, Andrés turned to his sister and hissed, 'You were damned well faking that illness. Don't deny it.'

She gave a beatific smile. 'I can deny whatever I like. What *you* can't deny is the spark between you. She's great.'

He glared at her.

'Andrés, she made you laugh. After the last couple of weeks you've had, you deserve some fun, and something tells me you'll have a lot more fun with Gabrielle than with me.'

If time wasn't so tight, he'd give his interfering sister a piece of his mind. He settled on another glare.

She waved cheerfully.

Setting off, he scrutinised the woman his sister had manipulated into taking as his replacement. Was she in on Sophia's Machiavellian plot? While he'd been learning from his lawyer that the world as he knew it hadn't ended after all, Sophia and Gabrielle had been chatting away like old friends.

It was the lack of guile in the returning stare, followed by her, 'Well come on then, palace etiquette. Unless you want me to embarrass you, tell me *everything*,' that sealed it for him.

'If in doubt, watch what I do and copy me, and you're going to make the muscles in your neck stiff if you don't relax.'

Gabrielle, who'd been listening intently to Andrés's rapidly delivered condensed palace etiquette tutorial, gave a surprised snigger. 'How can I relax in this thing? I'm frightened to touch anything in case I leave a mark.'

The car they were being chauffeured to the palace in was of a breed she was so used to seeing in the principality that she never even registered them other than to hope the gleaming monsters didn't knock her off her bicycle. The interior was as vast as she'd expected, smelling of leather and so shiny and sparkly that she could easily imagine being beamed up into space in it.

In answer, Andrés spread his hands and shrugged. 'It is a car, not a museum. Any marks will be cleaned.'

She'd never known people could live in such spotless fashion. His apartment had been just as immaculate as his car, not a speck of dust on any of the polished surfaces. No doubt he had a hidden army of minions emerging to spot clean the second a crumb was dropped. Andrés was immaculate too, from the perfectly quiffed black hair and the perfectly groomed thick black eyebrows to the perfectly trimmed thick black beard. Even his nails were buffed and trimmed to perfection. She'd guess no one had ever thought it necessary to order him to use a nail brush to scrub grime out from them. But then, she doubted he'd ever done a physical day's work in his life. She wondered if he worked out with people hovering beside him to wipe any sweat that dared pop out on his forehead.

There was a clear glass partition between them and the driver, but it had still been a relief that Andrés had kept close to the car door, legs stretched out, clearly making an effort to ensure distance and appear unthreatening despite his huge frame. What was less a relief was having to make a conscious effort not to stare at him. This was on top of dealing with the shame of her reaction to seeing him in his tuxedo. It had been a physical reaction her brain had had no control over and the only excuse she could come up with was that any woman would have looked at Andrés Morato filling a black tuxedo with a velvet lapel and sighed with pleasure. She guessed Sophia was too inured to the sight to bother sighing, not even an admiring glance of appreciation. Her attention had been all on Gabrielle, and it had been Gabrielle to whom she'd given the biggest embrace goodbye. Her lips had hardly grazed her husband's cheek when she'd seen them off into the limo. But then, Sophia was as beautiful as Andrés was handsome. She must be really secure in their marriage not to have any qualms about him spending the evening with another woman, even if that woman was a plain border guard with a small child, who needed an army of people working in tandem to make her presentable.

'What are you going to say when people ask why you're attending the party with someone who isn't your wife?'

His forehead creased with confusion. 'What are you talking about?'

'Sophia.'

His face contorted with what could only be described as grossed-out horror. 'Sophia isn't my wife. Sophia is my *sister.*'

Her heart slammed into her ribs. 'Your sister?'

'My sister.'

'But your surnames...'

The horror was replaced with disbelief. 'You speak my language better than most native speakers and deal with my compatriots every day at your border, and you don't know Spanish women keep their own names when they marry?'

'I...' Gabrielle tried to think coherently through the blood pounding in her brain. It hadn't occurred to her that the Moratos were anything but husband and wife. 'I've never really thought about it, and Sophia wears a wedding ring.'

'That's because she *is* married. Her husband's in New Zealand on business—he's a wine dealer. A simple internet search will confirm that I have no wife or partner, and for the avoidance of doubt, I have no intention of ever marrying.' His black stare bored into her. 'Is this a problem for you?'

'No, of course not,' she lied, even though she wasn't exactly sure why it was a lie. Nothing had changed as far as the party went. This wasn't a real date. She was still Sophia's substitute, accompanying Andrés only because there hadn't been time for him to arrange someone more fitting. 'I just thought you were married, that's all. It doesn't change anything.'

He held her stare another moment before giving a short, sharp nod. 'Good. Because we have arrived.'

Gabrielle blinked her gaze away from him—it was unnerving how staring into those black eyes made her feel all aflutter—and saw they were driving through the palace's famous arched gate built high into the ancient stone perimeter wall.

The car stopped and two members of the palace staff appeared and opened their respective doors for them.

Out on the gravelled stone of the huge courtyard, Gabrielle breathed the fresh sea air—the palace was built in the rocky shores of the Mediterranean overlooking its own private bay—deep into her lungs and took a moment to compose herself by taking in her surroundings. Her heartbeat was strangely erratic.

Andrés observed Gabrielle's stare fix on the huge fountain with the three marble horses rising majestically out of the water in the centre of the courtyard before her gaze lifted to take in the palace itself.

Now that he'd got over the ick factor of Gabrielle thinking he was married to his own sister, he found himself considering her reaction to it. It had put to rest the lingering doubt that she'd been a willing participant in his sister's matchmaking scheme. She'd been clearly mortified at having made the wrong assumption but he sensed something more than embarrassment had heated her cheeks enough to warm an igloo. Intriguing…

The last of the day's sun was landing like

microscopic jewels over her oval face and one bare shoulder, and when she turned her face to him and her oversized lips tugged into a hesitant small smile, the strangest frisson raced through his blood to imagine if those lips were as soft and pliant as they appeared.

One of the palace guards waiting for them cleared his throat loudly, snapping Andrés back to the present.

Shaking the strange frisson away, he indicated for Gabrielle to follow him to the main door.

As they were the last guests to arrive and he'd called ahead to notify the officials of the change to his plus one, they got through the security part quickly, and then they were led inside the palace itself. Having visited it a number of times since Catalina had taken the throne, Andrés's familiarity with the route they were taking and the lavishness of his own lifestyle meant the opulence of the palace was something he barely noticed. As such, when they followed the palace officials escorting them into a long, wide corridor, he'd taken a handful of steps over its deep blue carpet before he noticed that Gabrielle had dropped back.

Not just dropped back. She'd stopped walking altogether, her chin lifted and neck craning slowly about her, dark brown eyes wide with wonder as she soaked in the majesty surrounding them.

He strode back to her. 'I appreciate that this is your first time here but we have four minutes to take our seats before the banquet starts.'

Andrés's deeply masculine voice cut through Gabrielle's almost panicked stupor.

Never in her wildest dreams had she imagined she would one day find herself on the threshold of the famed Portrait Gallery, where the painted images of every single one of Monte Cleure's monarchs through the centuries lined the high walls. To be here, in the flesh, seconds away from sharing four walls with Queen Catalina...

The excitement and nerves churning in her stomach had become so violent that she could easily vomit over the deep blue carpet running the corridor's length.

She blinked vigorously, snatched as much air as she could get into her tight lungs, and met Andrés's black stare.

Surprisingly, sympathetic amusement tugged at his sensuous lips. 'The first time is always overwhelming.'

'Even for you?' She couldn't imagine this arrogant, confident man feeling overwhelmed by anything.

He raised his eyebrows pointedly. 'I don't

come from money, Gabrielle. I remember well the feeling I had in my stomach when I first joined this world. I was certain that people would take one look at me and judge me an imposter.'

She took in the immaculately groomed features of this devastatingly handsome man and the way his tuxedo wrapped around his fabulous body as if tuxedos had been designed with Andrés Morato in mind, and just could not imagine him ever doubting himself or his place in this world. 'How did you do it?'

'By telling myself that I could. I made a determined effort not to let my body language show my fear.'

'It worked?'

He raised a shoulder nonchalantly. 'We're here right now aren't we? And it can work for you too. You have an excellent poker face—'

'*Do I?*'

The way Gabrielle's face had scrunched up in disbelief amused Andrés. 'I spent the time you were searching my car wondering if you really were going to taser me.'

Her pillowy lips quirked. 'I was tempted.'

'I did wonder,' he said drily. 'And I would have deserved it. If you feel nerves getting the better of you, all you have to do is remember to breathe, hold your head high and put your poker face on.'

She considered this for a moment then sniffed through her slightly squished nose, lifted her chin and adopted a glazed expression like something out of a zombie movie. 'Like this?'

'That's not quite the poker face I remember,' he murmured, stifling a laugh.

Her cheeks sucked in as they'd done earlier when he'd suspected she was stifling her own laughter. 'I didn't even know I *had* a poker face.'

'You'll find it if you need it.' He held the crook of his arm out to her. 'Hold on to me for support and remember that you have nothing to fear. I promised my sister that I would take care of you and I never make promises I can't keep.'

Heart suddenly thumping again, Gabrielle hesitated a moment, not even knowing *why* she was hesitating when all he was doing was offering the support she needed, then slipped her hand as loosely as she could through his elbow. She fixed her gaze forwards, lifted her chin and tried to tune out the size of his bicep flexing against her fingers.

'Big breath,' he commanded.

She obeyed and was rewarded with a huge dose of his scent deep in her lungs. The only upside to that was her lungs gratefully opened up to receive the scent so she supposed being able to breathe semi-properly again was kind of a win, even if her heart was now smashing against her ribcage.

At the door of the busy banquet room, which Gabrielle was only able to get a tiny glimpse into, stood a makeshift archway elaborately decorated with roses. A photographer materialised.

'I'm afraid we're already late,' Andrés told him smoothly.

'The champagne reception has only just finished,' the photographer informed them. 'There is time before everyone takes their seats if we work quickly.'

Andrés's black stare landed on Gabrielle. She watched him deliberate in ultra-quick time then nod his assent.

In seconds, Gabrielle was taking her position beside Andrés under the arch.

'Closer together,' the photographer commanded.

All the breaths she'd managed to get back into her lungs rushed out of her when Andrés's arm slid behind her back and a giant hand rested on her hip.

Her heart thumped painfully against her already bruised ribcage, and she swallowed hard, as aware of the heat emanating from Andrés's huge frame pressed so tightly into her side as she was of the butterflies suddenly loose in her stomach. It took far more effort than should come naturally to bring a smile to her face.

The camera clicked, but there was no merciful release from Andrés's touch for he rested his hand on her lower back and steered her through the door into the banquet room.

Hundreds and hundreds of people dressed in the finest clothes money could buy were taking their seats. It wasn't until Gabrielle, trying valiantly to pretend that she wasn't in the slightest bit affected by Andrés's hand on her back, caught a glimpse of her heroine at the long top table that overlooked the dozens of round tables that she realised she'd completely forgotten all about the reason for the party.

'Did you just *squeal*?' Andrés asked in a low, astounded voice.

'I'm sorry,' she whispered, practically bouncing in excitement. 'I couldn't help it. I just spotted the Queen.'

Making a concerted effort not to look in the Queen's direction again so as not to embarrass herself again, Gabrielle flickered her eyes over the other guests and found herself having to clamp her lips together to stop another squeal escaping at all the faces she recognised. Anyone would recognise them. In this elaborately decorated banquet room, where light from gold and crystal chandeliers bounced off the oak floor and the beautifully laid tables, she recognised prime ministers and presidents, the bosses of multi-billion-dollar businesses, leading influencers and other faces she couldn't put a job or name to but whose faces were known around the world. Many of them were looking at her too, their faces drawn first to Andrés and then to his date, their expressions those of people trying to work out who she was. She wondered if any of the couples whose cars she'd searched earlier would recognise her now, in all Sophia's finery, and decided not. For some of them it was because they were too important in their own minds to look at the hoi polloi long enough for their faces to register, for the others it was just a stretch of the imagination too far. She wouldn't have believed it herself if it wasn't actually happening to her.

'Are you remembering to breathe?' Andrés enquired once they'd taken their seats, speaking close to Gabrielle's ear so only she could hear. The tip of his nose brushed against the strands of her hair and he suddenly found his senses filled with the contrasting scents of the musky perfume she'd chosen to spray herself with and the sweet shampoo she'd washed her hair with. *Dios*, the combination was temptation itself.

She nodded rigidly and after a beat turned to him. 'How's my poker face going?'

Her latest attempt reminded him of the victim of a zombie movie playing dead so they wouldn't get bitten. It was both amusing and yet strangely touching, and he reminded himself that this was Gabrielle's first foray into his world and that she'd had only hours to mentally prepare herself for it. He'd spent his entire life preparing for his first foray into this world.

'Terribly.' Keeping his voice low, he added, 'Just remember, every person in this room, including your Queen, has the same bodily functions as you and me.'

Her mouth dropped open in faux outrage and she leaned in closer to hiss, 'I do not want to think of Queen Catalina's bodily functions, thank you very much! I prefer to think of her as a mythical creature spreading goodwill and hope amongst her subjects, so do not ruin my illusions by humanising her for me.'

Staring into dark brown eyes dancing with amusement, Andrés caught another waft of her perfume. It was a familiar scent but the way it reacted to Gabrielle's skin...

Something stirred inside him, a tightening, a flicker of heat that was only partially broken a beat later when the waiting staff descended. They filled the smallest of the crystal glasses set out before them, little bigger than his thumb, with amber liquid.

Gabrielle picked hers up and sniffed it gingerly. It smelt sweet. Safe. Because sniffing the sweet liquid meant she wasn't inhaling the scent of Andrés.

She could still feel the tiny quivering tendrils that had formed at the roots of her hair when he'd spoken into her ear. Still feel the whisper of his warm breath on her lobe.

'It's the pre-banquet drink; a form of sherry,' he explained. 'In a moment we will all stand and drink the first toast to the Queen's health.'

No sooner had he spoken than a glass was tapped.

Chairs scraped back as all the guests got to their feet. Gabrielle rose in time with Andrés, completely forgetting that heeled shoes reacted differently to being stood up in than clumpy boots. Losing her balance, she swung her arm out, instinctively grabbed his hand and swayed into him.

CHAPTER FOUR

IF ANDRÉS WASN'T so strong Gabrielle would have sent them both sprawling. As it was, he was not only strong but had superb reflexes and instincts. Long, warm fingers wrapped around Gabrielle's and squeezed, the solid muscle of the shoulder her cheek landed on not giving way an inch.

Heart pounding wildly, wholly aware that the tip of her breast was squashed into his forearm and mortified at how close she'd come to embarrassing them both, she took a deep breath and adjusted her stance.

It frightened her how badly her hand wanted to stay in his, frightened her even more that when she pulled it free her hand refused to make a quick release, their fingers drifting apart like a caress.

The whole thing lasted seconds. It felt like for ever.

'Sorry,' she whispered.

'Don't be,' he murmured.

The toast to the Queen's health was made. The whooshing of blood in Gabrielle's ears drowned it out completely.

She didn't dare look at Andrés. Not a part of her didn't tingle. How she hadn't spilled her drink everywhere was a mystery she would never solve but she gladly drank it in one swallow when the command was given. Not strong enough to burn but potent enough to take the edge off her nerves. It barely touched the tingles.

She was only having them because, outside of work, she was starved for adult company and, she could admit, more than a little lonely, so was it really a surprise that she should develop an attraction to the first reasonably handsome man to stray in her path?

She nearly laughed out loud at the understatement of her thoughts. *Reasonably* handsome? Andrés would give Zeus an inferiority complex.

What she needed to do, Gabrielle decided, was accept that she was attracted to Andrés, accept that learning he wasn't actually married had accelerated it, and park it. Enjoy the party that she was the luckiest woman in Monte Cleure to be attending and enjoy the company of her handsome date on what wasn't a real date in the real sense because if it was, she wouldn't have agreed to it and he certainly wouldn't have suggested it. Glamorous men like Andrés Morato liked glamorous women with matching glamorous lives, not ordinary, squat border guards. You didn't live in the principality of Monte Cleure your entire life without learning that. Once the evening was over, she would never see him again. He'd forget about her in days. Probably hours. Most likely by the time his car had turned around after dropping her home.

And she'd return to the beautiful boy she'd given her life to protect, and forget all about him.

Andrés swallowed his pre-dinner drink and turned his attention to Gabrielle. Not that his attention had left her. Awareness was thrumming through him at a rate he could scarcely believe, and all because she'd stumbled into him and grabbed his hand for support and the soft swell of her breast had pressed against his arm, accelerating the awareness that had already been building.

Something in the way she was holding herself and the way her teeth were sinking into her bottom lip made him think the awareness wasn't entirely one-sided.

As they retook their seats, the waiting staff arrived with the bread rolls. Andrés cut straight into his, slathered one half with a pat of butter, and took a huge bite. It had been a long day and he'd hardly eaten. He was ravenous.

Taking another huge bite, he watched Gabrielle butter her own roll and idly wondered if her golden skin matched it for soft smoothness. Wondered what it tasted like…

Her face turned to his and she casually—too casually?—asked, 'Which wine should I have? White or red?'

He spread another pat of butter on the other half of his roll. 'Whichever you like.'

'But I don't really like wine,' she confessed, making a face that matched her dislike of it. 'Some friends and I shared a bottle years ago— it tasted like drain cleaner.'

The way she said it made him want to laugh. 'I am sure you will find the wine here infinitely more palatable.'

'I hope that's the case because I don't really think it's the done thing for guests to be sick over the silk tablecloths.' And then, with a gleam of amusement, her delightful pillowy lips closed over her own roll.

Grinning at her irreverence, he nodded at the approaching wine servers. 'It's time to decide.'

She swallowed her mouthful and pulled another face. 'I'll let you decide, and if it's horrible and I'm sick, you can take the blame.'

Andrés didn't know if it was the face she'd pulled or what she'd said or how she'd said it, but the laughter he'd been holding back escaped.

His sister had been right. Gabrielle had made him laugh earlier and she was making him laugh now. He had a feeling that even if the legal issues with Susi hadn't been resolved earlier that day, Gabrielle's company would still have lightened the tightness that lived in his chest during those torrid weeks, because he was feeling lighter than he'd done in a long, long time.

Choosing red for them both, he watched Gabrielle sniff hers suspiciously like she'd done with the pre-dinner drink.

'If you don't like it, we'll get something else brought over for you,' he assured her.

Her nose wrinkled. 'It doesn't smell offensive.'

'I should hope not,' he observed, smothering another laugh. Raising his glass, he held it out to her. *'Salud.'*

She tapped her glass to it. *'Santé.'*

Her lips pulled in as she swirled the red liquid around her mouth before taking another, larger, drink.

'More palatable than the drain cleaner?' he asked, even though the wonder in her eyes already told him the answer.

She swallowed another sip and shook her head. 'That is…' She put her glass on the table and pinched her forefingers and thumbs together into circles.

Gabrielle's tongue was rhapsodising. She'd never known wine could be so smooth. It was easily the most delicious thing she had ever tasted…right up until the scallops with crispy pancetta were served…and then a lemon sorbet palate cleanser…

She was in heaven! She demolished every last morsel, delighted to have her attention and senses filled with the wonderful aroma and taste of food rather than Andrés. Not that she'd tasted him of course, and she quickly drank some wine to counter the thrill that zinged through her to wonder what his lips tasted of.

By enthusiastically concentrating on the fabulous food, Gabrielle was able to push any Andrés effect away and just enjoy herself as she'd already determined to do, and she quickly relaxed into the meal and her surroundings. She would have been happy to just listen in on the conversations washing around her but Andrés made sure to include her in it all. It didn't escape her attention that he instinctively seemed to know which subjects, like the German stock market, meant nothing to her and leaned his head close to hers to give a quick, discreet summary under his breath. While those discreet summaries kept recharging the Andrés effect, she was touched and grateful for his consideration. Her short time working at the casino that boasted the highest percentage of the world's billionaires in its membership had taught her that many men in his situation wouldn't care if their date could keep up with the conversation, never mind go out of their way to include her in it. They'd be too puffed up with the sound of their own voices to even care.

'So what is it you do?' the forty-something white-blonde lady sitting on the other side of Andrés asked Gabrielle in English after the third course had been cleared away and the table conversation had come to a natural break.

Gabrielle, who'd just dropped the velvet place setting with her name embroidered in gold thread into her clutch bag and was pondering how to pilfer her personalised place menu, shot her gaze to Andrés with a sinking dread in her stomach.

How did he want her to handle this? She didn't want to lie—she'd told so many lies since the pregnancy that if heaven existed she'd be barred from entering—but she didn't want to embarrass him either.

His eyes caught hers before the faintest of smiles played on his lips and he said in perfect English, 'Gabrielle is a border guard.'

Only by the skin of her teeth did she stop her mouth dropping open. The last thing she'd expected was for Andrés to tell the truth, not because she assumed he was a natural born liar but because she'd assumed he would think it beneath him to admit he'd brought along a no-body to an event with the world's elite.

Another assumption she'd got wrong.

The woman slapped his arm. 'You are such a tease, Andrés.'

'I'm not teasing. Gabrielle stopped my car at the Spanish border earlier and searched it for drugs.' He lifted his glass to his mouth. 'Gabrielle will confirm it,' he added before dropping her a wink that made her stomach dip.

'It is true,' she piped up, speaking carefully as her English wasn't as fluent as her Spanish. 'I work as border guard. Andrés fitted the...' She grasped for the translation of *profile* but came up blank. '...details we were given of a drug smuggler bringing cocaine over the border. I am here only because Sophia fell ill. I am the substitute.'

The woman pouted. 'Oh, you're as bad as he is.'

Gabrielle met Andrés's stare. The conspiratorial crinkling of his eyes and flash of perfect teeth made her stomach dip again even more powerfully, as did the frankly shocking realisation that she could perfectly read in his expression that he found the blonde woman ridiculous.

He moved a touch closer to her and, switching back to Spanish, murmured, 'You wait, Lucida will spend the rest of the evening trying to get to the bottom of who you really are.'

'Lucida? She was named after a *font*?'

Surprise lit his face and then he gave such a deep throated rumble of laughter that everyone surrounding them whipped their stares to him.

It was laughter that, despite the tight control she was keeping over her reactions to him, made Gabrielle's heart swell.

He moved his face even closer and dropped his voice even lower. 'Legend has it that she changed it from Lucinda. Someone told her it sounded classier.'

'I take it that someone was having a joke?'

'I believe that is a fair assumption.'

Luckily their next course arrived, saving either of them from having to explain what it was that had them both laughing and saving Gabrielle from the effects of Andrés's breath whispering against her temple.

A large sip of wine in an attempt to mute the awareness whooshing around her body, and then she popped a crispy potato ball with the fluffiest inside into her mouth. That was better, even if she was acutely aware of the closeness of his thigh under the table. Still, she told herself, a bit of internal discomfort was nothing when she was eating food fit for a princess and drinking wine that Zeus himself would have declared all the superlatives. And thinking of Zeus, Gabrielle was starting to understand that there was far more to Andrés than his devastating looks. He wore his arrogance like a cloak but he wasn't a snob and actually had a sense of humour, something she would never have believed five hours ago. With the crispiest pork crackling in the whole world dissolving on her tongue, all she could think was that for this one night, she was the luckiest woman in the world. To think she'd thought the highlight of her evening would be a bath!

'Can I ask you something personal?' he asked as the last of the crackling dissolved into nothing.

The old internal alarm system went off. Choosing her words carefully, she said, 'You can ask but I might choose not to answer.'

'That is fair. I'm just wondering why you do the work you do.'

She narrowed her eyes to scrutinise him, wondering where this was leading. 'That is a strange way to phrase it.'

His broad shoulders rose as he drank some of his wine. 'See, this is why I'm asking. You are clearly educated. You speak three languages...'

'French is my native language and all Monte Cleure children are taught English and Spanish at school,' she interjected. 'It is nothing special.'

'You speak my language as well as I do and your English is excellent.'

She felt her cheeks flush with pleasure at the compliment. Spanish had always come easily to her but English was *hard*.

'You must have studied hard to be as proficient as you are at them,' he continued. 'Then there is the way you speak, your knowledge of fonts.' He pulled an amazed face. 'Come on, who knows about fonts?'

'I do. You do.'

'I know about fonts because I own Janson Media.'

'The TV company?'

'We also publish newspapers and magazines.' He named a few that made her eyes widen. 'When I buy into a company I want to know everything about it.'

'And that meant learning about *fonts*?'

He grinned. 'I can be obsessive. Also, it was the first major company I bought into—they were struggling to transition into the digital age and the shares were going cheap enough to entice me. I'm now the majority shareholder. Funnily enough, I'm currently going through the process of buying a Japanese publishing company. I've wanted to break into the Asian market for a long time and this is the first real viable option for me, but going back to you, Gabrielle, you are an intelligent woman. I cannot believe a career as a border guard is what you dreamed for yourself.'

And she couldn't believe he'd tapped into her so easily. She couldn't decide if it was terrifying or enthralling, knew only that the beats of her heart were racing at a canter. 'It isn't what I dreamed of doing,' she agreed, forcing herself to speak calmly. Just because Andrés had picked up on certain things about her in the short space of time they'd spent together did not mean he could actually read her mind. 'But then, I never imagined I would have a child at nineteen.'

'What career did you dream of?'

'Publishing. Books,' she hastened to clarify, not wanting him to think she was only saying it because he'd mentioned he owned a media company and was in the process of buying another. 'I had a place at a university in England to study English Literature lined up.'

Andrés was impressed. He could never understand people who were content to limit their horizons to the places of their birth. 'Publishing is wide ranging. What did you want to do within it?'

'I hadn't decided. I just liked the idea of being absorbed into the world of words. I was going to do my degree and then see where it led me. My mother is a reader. We never had much money but there were always books at home. You could open one and be transported to any place in time anywhere in the world.'

'What stopped you pursuing your dream?'

She pulled a 'duh' face. 'I told you, I had a baby. I couldn't go to university in another country with a baby in tow. It just wasn't feasible even if I could have afforded it, and Monte Cleure doesn't have a university, and there is no point in me bewailing it because I made my choice and that choice was Lucas. I won't lie, being a border guard isn't the career I once dreamed of but it's a living and one I'm proud of, and it has a career ladder I can climb as Lucas gets older and becomes less dependent on me.'

'I'm not criticising you,' he said, noting the defensiveness in the rapidity of her speech. 'Being a parent means making sacrifices and I have nothing but admiration for the people who are prepared to make them.'

Something flickered in her eyes, an emotion he couldn't discern but which strangely tugged at his chest. Gabrielle had been so young when she'd had her child that he could only imagine the other sacrifices she'd had to make. 'I know you said it was just you and Lucas but is his father on the scene?'

The colour that suffused her face was so different to the colour it had turned when she'd learned that Sophia wasn't his wife that he immediately regretted asking. 'That is none of my business. I apologise. Forget I asked.'

She had a long drink of her water. 'No, it's okay. And no, he isn't on the scene at all. It's been just me and Lucas since the day I brought him home.' The pillowy lips he was finding it harder and harder not to fantasise about the taste and feel of curved into a smile that didn't quite meet her eyes. 'And as we're speaking of Lucas, does your jacket have an inside pocket?'

Her change of subject threw him. 'Why do you ask?'

'I want to sneak my place menu out as a memento for him but the bag Sophia lent me is so small I'm scared I'll damage it.'

Gabrielle held her breath as she waited for him to respond, and she mentally kicked herself for not giving him the pat response she'd honed over the years to explain The Bastard's absence to the curious, which consisted of Lucas's father being a tourist she'd had a brief fling with and that he'd given her a fake number and so she'd never been able to tell him of their son. She'd repeated the lie so many times it came naturally to her. What wasn't natural was her tongue's refusal to repeat that lie to Andrés.

After what felt like an age in which the black

stare she was finding increasingly hypnotic bored into her, the sides of his eyes crinkled. A giant hand reached across her empty plate. The sleeves of his jacket and shirt pulled back, revealing the fine dark hair covering his arm and the base of his sleeve tattoo. A place deep and low between her legs pulsed. A moment later her place menu was swallowed into the mysterious confines of Andrés dinner jacket.

'If I get thrown in the dungeon for theft, I will expect you to plead my case for me,' he said in the lighter tone of their earlier conversation.

'I will get down on my knees before my Queen and beg for your mercy,' she agreed, laughing at both the absurdity and the relief that came with the complete change of subject.

Over the next two courses, Gabrielle stuck to water while they ate and chatted. She was making herself ration the wine. She drank alcohol so rarely that the last thing she wanted was to get drunk and make a fool of herself. Besides, she didn't need alcohol. She was high enough on the buzz being induced by the whole evening and, she had to admit, the buzz that came from being the sole focus of Andrés's attention.

Something was happening inside her, butterflies multiplying and growing in wing strength, but so long as she didn't look at him too hard or let his scent seep into her airwaves and so long as she completely tuned out the closeness of his body next to hers and didn't look at his arm—she had no idea why she should react to an *arm* of all things—she was able to temper the Andrés effect and just enjoy talking to him. But temper it only slightly. She doubted there was a woman alive who wouldn't react to being in close proximity to such a rampantly masculine man whom even Zeus would be jealous of.

She could scarcely believe that the arrogant, entitled jerk who'd practically had a tantrum at having his car searched was someone she actually liked. She would never have believed such a man could be so easy to talk to or that she could be so enthralled listening to his tales. He was only ten years older than her but had lived, truly *lived*, enough to have five decades on her.

To learn he'd founded his multi-billion business empire out of nothing blew her mind.

'I thought you were just trying to calm my nerves when you said you didn't come from money,' she confessed after he'd explained how he'd signed himself up for a distance-learning business degree whilst still studying at school *and* worked weekends as a barista and how, once he'd saved twenty thousand euros by the age of twenty, he'd invested it in two start-up companies founded by school friends which had both struck gold.

'I *was* trying to calm you,' he said with the sensuous smile that had made her stomach dip more times than she could count that evening. 'But it also happened to be the truth.'

'Where do you get your *drive* from?' she marvelled. The hours he worked, the relentless travel...

She liked that he didn't give her a pat answer. Liked that he considered the question before answering. 'It's something that has always been in me. It runs in my family—Sophia has the same drive. Our parents are both hard workers but the money they earned was hardly enough to keep the wolves from the door. I always wanted to be rich and so I made it happen.'

'Does that always happen for you?' she asked, fascinated. 'Do you always get what you want?'

Gabrielle suddenly found herself holding her breath as his face drew closer to hers. The swirl in his hypnotic black eyes deepened and pulsed as the sensuous lips her eyes were increasingly drawn to parted. *'Always.'*

CHAPTER FIVE

THE REST OF the party attendees had ceased to exist for Andrés.

The longer the meal went on, the more he was reminded of long ago years, when he'd been too young for any lover to expect anything but fun from him, before he'd found himself approaching relationships wondering when he would be forced to end it. He'd learned to be forthright, firmly stating at the outset that he would never settle down or marry and while they always—*always*—reacted with a nonchalant shrug, each of them managed to convince themselves that they would be the one to change him, to make him fall in love. As if love even existed beyond the bonds forged by blood! His parents had believed they loved each other once but before their children reached double digits had become incapable of holding a conversation without dripping poison into it.

The moment marriage was hinted at, he ended it. Same as when lovers 'accidentally' left their toothbrush in his bathroom. Experience had taught him that ignoring those hints and letting things drag on until boredom kicked in meant a messy disentanglement. None had been messier than with Susi, the woman responsible for the dark cloud that had hung over him these last weeks.

The call from his lawyer had lifted that cloud. Having Gabrielle as his date for the evening had blown the last of it away completely.

Other than her relative youth, Gabrielle was nothing like those young, carefree lovers of his early twenties, but there was something about her that reminded him of that time, before life had made him so cynical, a time before he'd become jaded with humans in general. A time when he'd woken each day enthusiastic for what lay ahead.

He'd known she was different from his usual dates and lovers when he'd agreed with Sophia's suggestion that Gabrielle be her substitute for the evening. The fact of her child had sold it for him. A woman with her own life and responsibilities and who lived in such a vastly different world to his wouldn't view him with long-term grasping eyes. When the evening had begun, Gabrielle hadn't wanted or expected anything from Andrés other than to be delivered safely home at the end of it.

And now…?

Call him arrogant but Andrés knew when a woman was attracted to him. It was all the little signs and Gabrielle was displaying them in abundance. What made it more erotic though, was his certainty that she was unaware of the signals she was giving. She couldn't know that her beautiful dark brown eyes had melted into a bar of the most luxurious of chocolate or that her body was subtly leaning towards him, or that her face was constantly tilted to his.

He was coming to think Gabrielle might just be the most interesting and intriguing woman he'd ever spent time with. She had that rare combination of seriousness and intelligence coupled with a mischievous joy of the absurd that was sexy in its own right, and when the sixth course was cleared away, he put his elbow on the table, rested his chin on his closed fist and drank her in some more. She was *extraordinary*.

Taking a sip of what was only her second glass of wine, she studied him meditatively before putting her own elbow on the table and resting her chin on the palm of her hand. Her hair spilled over her shoulder. 'Can I ask *you* something personal?'

'I think that is only fair but the same rules apply.'

She smiled slowly. 'Of course.'

The heat in his veins thickened some more. Their faces were only inches from each other...

'Why were you in such a bad mood earlier?'

'I didn't think you'd noticed,' he jested even as his heart sank. Andrés had hoped to get through this evening without having to think about the nightmare he'd just been through.

'Don't worry,' she jested back, 'it wasn't particularly obvious.'

He grinned ruefully and studied her with the same meditation with which she'd studied him. For a moment he debated whether or not to enforce the 'choosing not to answer' clause they'd already agreed on. 'I've been embroiled in a paternity battle.'

A dark brown eyebrow arched.

'A woman I dated briefly for a month last year got in touch a few weeks ago and told me I was the father of her child.'

'And were you—are you—the father?'

He shook his head emphatically. 'No. I knew the child couldn't be mine. It wasn't possible. A DNA test confirmed it. My lawyer called me with the results when you were searching my car.'

She moved her hand from her chin, sitting back a little from him, and rubbed her arm. 'Was it the thought of being a father that put you in such a foul temper?'

'No… Yes. But not for the reasons you think.'

Her eyebrow arched again. 'You can read my mind?'

'Unfortunately all the riches in the world doesn't bestow that power.' He grabbed the back of his neck and wished that he could read her mind. It was one thing discussing these matters dispassionately with his legal team but Gabrielle had a child she was raising without the father's involvement. For all that she refused to *bewail* the choices she'd made, he didn't imagine life was easy for her.

'Gabrielle, I like children—I'm godfather to my cousin's sons and I very much enjoy the time I spend with them—but I don't want to get married or be stuck with a long-term partner, and having children means I would be stuck in a potentially toxic relationship. I couldn't be like Lucas's father. I would want to be there every day for my child, just as my father was for me, but my parents' marriage is toxic and I have never wanted that for myself.' He drained his wine and shook his head. 'I can barely remember a time when they didn't hate each other but they stayed together for mine and Sophia's sake and now I think they enjoy hating each other so much that they stay together out of spite.'

'That sounds horrible but there's no reason any marriage you made would go the same way.' She shrugged her shoulders lightly. 'My parents' marriage was happy.'

'Was?'

Sadness clouded her stare. 'My father died when I was ten. Sepsis.'

He gave a grim shake of his head. 'I'm sorry,' he said, meaning it. Divorce had been Andrés's biggest fear at that age. He couldn't begin to imagine how he'd have coped if either of his parents had died, and a sharp pang sliced his chest to think how much he'd neglected them in recent years. It wasn't deliberate, merely that all his business interests meant there weren't enough hours in the day for anything other than business.

'Thank you. It's been thirteen years but I still miss him. My mother does too. Losing him devastated her.' Her shoulders rose again and she softly added, 'Not all marriages end in acrimony.'

They were words he'd heard before, from countless lovers. Usually they sent alarm bells clanging and sent Andrés heading swiftly to the nearest exit, but on this occasion he sensed they came from a thoughtful place, not a self-serving one.

'I know that but when you've lived through a toxic marriage, life is too short to take the risk. If Susi's child had been mine I have no doubt it would have turned toxic between us quickly.'

'How can you be so certain?'

'She took a baseball bat to my Maserati when I ended things. She smashed all the windows and the bonnet. She was trying to smash her way into the garage to get to the other cars when my security apprehended her.'

Gabrielle's eyes had widened, shock ringing loud and clear. 'After you'd been together only a month?'

'Yes. And it was never serious. I saw her maybe five times in that month.'

'That is not someone who sounds stable.'

'Exactly. It is why I ended things with her. I was getting some serious bad vibes. When she told me I was the father, I knew she was lying. I am scrupulous about contraception.'

'That poor baby,' she said with a hint of distress.

'Don't worry about the baby,' he assured her. Not even Sophia, the only person outside his legal team he'd confided the situation to, had mentioned any concerns for Susi's child. 'I've had business dealings with Susi's father and I spoke to him and Grace, Susi's mother, when she first made the claims. They know their daughter needs help and they've promised me they will give it to her.'

Her features relaxed at this. Putting her chin back on her hand, she murmured with more of that husky softness, 'That's good. And good of you to think to do that.'

Andrés actually felt his chest expand. Why a woman he'd known barely a quarter of a day's opinion mattered he couldn't begin to explain but there were a lot of things about this woman and the things he was confiding and the way he was reacting to her that couldn't be rationalised.

At that moment, a server reached between them to lay the plates of their seventh and penultimate course down, and Andrés experienced a stab of resentment at being prevented from looking at Gabrielle for all of ten seconds.

It was her eyes he realised a few moments later when they each lifted a spoonful of warm lemon tart to their mouths and their gazes were drawn back together. They were so expressive and warm and open that it was impossible for a man to look into them and not feel the urge to spill his soul...

Incapable of pulling her stare away from Andrés, Gabrielle inhaled the scent of her beautifully presented individual tart that smelt as if the lemons had been picked only minutes ago and thought that as beautiful as its aroma was, it could never smell as good as him. Nothing could.

Muting the Andrés effect had become impossible. The constant fluttering in her chest and the churning sick-like feeling in her stomach had grown so strong it was a struggle to swallow the dessert that tasted as good as its scent promised.

Would he be having such a stark effect on her if she'd let her brother fix her up with his friends like he'd pestered over the years? Hadn't he told her more times than she could count that committing herself to a life of celibacy went against every human instinct and craving?

Gabrielle's deep, abiding love for Lucas and profound terror of losing him had allowed her to ignore her brother's wisdom. And besides, how, she'd asked herself, could she miss something she'd never had?

It was pointless to wonder. That the Andrés effect was strong was one of only two certainties she had because she knew she wasn't imagining that the attraction was mutual. She was inexperienced but not naive. With every passing minute she could feel the charge between them growing, a thought that thrilled and terrified her in equal measure.

She'd made a promise. A vow. No relationships. Just her and Lucas. The risks of giving herself to a man were just too strong.

But Andrés's heaven-sent scent and the pull of those sensuous lips…

'Tell me about your life,' Andrés said once the coffees had been poured and they'd both demolished a delicate *petit four* each.

He could watch Gabrielle talk for ever. There

was something about the way her mouth and face moved when she spoke that fascinated him. A deep thrum pulsed relentlessly through his thickened veins to imagine what those oversized lips would feel like crushed against his mouth.

As if she could sense the direction of his thoughts, her fingers flew to her mouth and rubbed gently against it. He was quite sure she was unaware of doing it.

'What do you want to know?'

'I don't know… What is a typical day in the life of Gabrielle Breton?'

'I suppose a typical working day starts with early morning cartoons and breakfast, then a fight with Lucas over wearing more than a pair of pants, then I drop him either at nursery or if my shift's over the weekend at my mother's, and work until my shift finishes and then collect him, go back home to throw something together for dinner, kick a ball about in the park—my brother has taught Lucas the joy of soccer and I'm now required to be the goalkeeper and have balls kicked at my face every day—and then I wrestle him into his pyjamas, read him a story and then bed.' Her nose wrinkled and then her mesmerising eyes gleamed. 'I bet it's very different to a typical day in the life of Andrés Morato.'

'Just a little bit,' he admitted with a laugh,

thinking of the few times his godsons had talked him into playing soccer with them. Another sharp pang pulled at his chest to remember he hadn't seen them since Christmas.

Gabrielle's oh-so-interesting, beautiful face lit up with a mischievous smile. 'Yours is a life of glamour and travel while mine is a life of domestic drudgery and the vain hope on a work shift of actually catching some smug billionaire with a large haul of drugs.'

'Am I still included in your smug billionaire hit list?'

Her delicious pillowy lips pursed in pretend concentration before she grinned. 'I think we can safely let you go back to using facial recognition. After all, you're a very busy and important man who pumps a lot of money into my country's economy. I would hate to delay you on your important business.'

He adopted a deliberately smug expression. 'Now you are thinking in the correct way.'

'One evening with a billionaire and I'm already corrupted.' Amusement dancing in her eyes, she lazily brought her coffee cup to her mouth. 'By the time you take me home I'll be stamping my feet at the unfairness of not having my own staff to help with all the chores.'

'To *help* with the chores?' He shook his head

in faux disappointment. 'If you are going to employ staff it is to do the chores for you.'

Her left eyebrow rose and wriggled. '*All* the chores?'

He raised his right eyebrow in imitation. 'I am a very busy and important man.'

She put her cup and saucer back on the table without breaking the lock of their eyes. 'I'm surprised you haven't already mentioned that.'

'Modesty forbade it.'

'I would say you should give classes in modesty but your time is precious. I bet you don't even have time to make yourself a snack when you're hungry.'

'I poured my own bourbon while I waited for you to finish getting ready earlier. Does that count?'

Her laughter whooshed through his ears and seeped into his veins. Gabrielle's laughter was the definition of sexy.

'When was the last time you did your own laundry?' she challenged teasingly.

'What is laundry?' he joked, to more of that glorious laughter.

'The last time you dusted?'

He wondered if she was aware of the lock of hair she was winding around her finger. 'I have a vague idea of where the cleaning items are stored in all of my homes if that counts?'

Gabrielle was laughing so hard that she didn't hear the call for the final toast of the evening to the Queen. It was only as fresh champagne flutes were delivered to their table and everyone around them started rising to their feet that she realised what was happening and followed suit.

'If you stumble again, you are more than welcome to fall into me,' Andrés's deep voice murmured close to her ear.

Blood whooshed straight to her brain, its strength making her sway on her feet.

As with the first toast, Gabrielle didn't hear a single word. It was impossible with the roaring in her head. It didn't help that Andrés's arm was brushed against hers. Or was it her arm brushed against his…?

There had been no mistaking the suggestive undertone in his words. No mistaking the first verbal acknowledgement of the attraction that had seen them spend the vast majority of the banquet ignoring everyone around them, and her cheeks heated to realise she'd been flirting with him. Teasing him. Completely wrapped up with him. The signals she must have been giving out…

Oh, God, did this mean he thought…?

Her breaths were short and her legs decidedly shaky when she retook her seat, and she edged her chair away from his, taking a moment to breathe and collect herself by checking her phone for any messages. Her mother had sent her a picture of Lucas sleeping in Romeo's arms.

That helped hugely. A picture of her cherubic son was just the tonic she needed to counter the heady thickness in her veins and the smashing of her heart against her ribs.

She'd just responded with a melting heart emoji when an arm slid around the back of her chair and the sleeve of Andrés's tuxedo tickled against her neck. Before she could think to react, a warm cheek pressed against hers and the soft bristles of Andrés's beard were grazing against her skin.

All the air flew out of her lungs while simultaneously her pelvis flamed and contracted, warmth gushing through her like a tsunami.

'That has to be your brother,' he said, peering at her screen. 'He looks just like you. And is that your son?'

Gabrielle had to swallow the moisture that had flooded her mouth. All she could manage was a short nod.

'He's beautiful,' he observed huskily.

Suddenly she found she didn't dare move a muscle. When she did manage a response, her voice sounded distant, like it belonged to someone else. 'I like to think so too.'

Mercifully, an official called for everyone's attention and announced the party would be moving to the ballroom.

At least she thought it was merciful timing until the tip of Andrés's nose dragged along her cheekbone, the sleeve of his arm slid in reverse and then the heat of his face against hers and the heat of his body was gone.

How was it possible to be both relieved and internally screaming in disappointment at the same time and over the same thing?

There was still a little champagne left from the toast in her flute, and she knocked it back before summoning the courage to meet Andrés's stare.

He'd already risen, his black stare penetrating down at her.

The dip in her stomach was so powerful it would have knocked her off her feet if she'd been standing.

Without saying a word, he extended a giant hand to her.

With no knowledge of allowing them to do so, her trembling fingers reached out to take it. Long fingers wrapped around them and then Gabrielle was being gently helped to her feet, which was just as well as her legs had turned to wobbly water.

Upright, gazing into Andrés's face, as aware

of the inherent masculinity that breathed in his huge frame as she'd ever been, more aware of her own contrasting femininity than she'd ever been before, aware her cheeks were drenched in hot colour, for one thrilling, terrifying moment, time ceased.

And then air forced its way into her lungs and her head cleared enough for her to regain enough sense to move back a little, just enough to stop the heat of his body penetrating her in the same way his hypnotic eyes were. It made no difference. The cells of her body were still straining towards him. Her effort to remove her hand from his clasp was a failure too, her fingers absolutely refusing to cooperate.

'What comes next?' she asked in a voice that still sounded like it belonged to someone else, then felt more hot colour suffuse her cheeks at how her question could be interpreted and almost tripped over her own tongue to add, 'I mean with the party.'

The black eyes gleamed and the lips she kept fighting to stop herself from imagining kissing quirked at the sides. 'Dancing and cocktails.' With another gleam of his eyes, he released her hand and held the crook of his arm out. 'Shall we?'

Feeling like she'd slipped into a dream, Gabrielle slipped her hand into it, just as she'd done over four hours earlier. Except, those few hours earlier her legs had been shaking with excitement, her physical awareness of Andrés in its infancy.

If she'd known how quickly and deeply that awareness would mushroom, she'd have pretended to have caught Sophia's bug.

But she couldn't have known. Couldn't have *imagined*.

Nothing could happen, she told herself desperately as her senses were once again filled entirely with Andrés. So filled were they as they joined the exodus from the banquet room to the ballroom that she barely registered the French actor they passed whose posters she'd plastered all over her teenage bedroom or noticed when she was within arm's reach of the Queen.

If you stumble again, you are more than welcome to fall into me.

Those words had let the Genie out of the bottle, and Gabrielle quivered inside to remember the suggestiveness of his undertone and the seductive sensuousness that had laced it.

Until he'd said those words she'd been fully aware of the growing attraction between them, of course she had, as aware as she'd ever been of anything in her life, but she'd been able to contain it by the skin of her teeth. Saying those words, bringing it out into the open for the first time…

And then that caress of his cheek against hers. She didn't think she could have reacted more strongly if he'd kissed her, which was the wrong thing to think as now she was thinking about his sensuous lips again and her pelvis was contracting painfully… No, not painfully. The ache deep within her wasn't pain.

The myriad of waiting staff now carried trays of tall cocktail glasses filled to the brim with colourful liquid, and Gabrielle gladly helped herself to a pink one and drank deeply through its straw. So wrapped up were her thoughts on Andrés that she barely tasted it, and whatever alcohol it contained did nothing to help.

Unexpected help though, came from two couples of around Andrés's age who beetled over to them. Before she knew what was happening, Gabrielle had been forced to disentangle her hand from his elbow so they could both be enveloped in embraces and air kisses. The banter and familiarity amongst them made it obvious that these were his friends, not just acquaintances, and when names of introduction were thrown at her, she was too busy alternating between the relief of being part of a pack and no longer the sole focus of Andrés's attention, and longing for him to steer her away to a private table for two to listen properly.

Heaven help her, as desperately as she knew nothing could happen between them, already she wanted time to reverse back to the banquet and those magical hours when it had felt like she and Andrés were the only two people in the world. Back to those magical hours before he'd let the Genie out and Gabrielle had realised just how much danger she was in.

CHAPTER SIX

THE ATMOSPHERE IN the ballroom was dramatically different to the formality of the banquet room. The room itself was twice its size and positively oozed glamour, the disco music pumping out and the effects of multiple disco balls hanging from the impossibly high ceiling giving it a real retro vibe.

An abundance of round tables encircled the sprawling dance floor, and when the group bagged one as a base, Gabrielle copied the other women in throwing her clutch bag onto it then helped herself to another pink cocktail. She was sure her tongue should be rhapsodising about it as it had done with the wine but her tastebuds seemed to have gone on strike.

The dance floor was already half filled with people shaking their moves and she gladly followed the women of their newly formed group onto it, leaving the men to continue whatever they were discussing.

She sensed Andrés's gaze following her every step.

It took all her willpower not to look back at him.

The physical space away from him was just what she needed and, in the company of women who were clearly on a mission to party the night away, she made sure to position herself with her back to the tables. After forcefully reminding herself that she would never again be invited to dance in the palace ballroom, she danced like she hadn't danced since she was an adolescent. Which wasn't hard as she hadn't actually danced at all since she was eighteen and had found Eloise collapsed in distress in the family bathroom on the night of what should have been Gabrielle's prom.

Ignoring the ache in her feet, which were practically begging for mercy from the elegant heels she'd forced them in, she threw herself into the music. Her body was desperate for an outlet for all the Andrés induced feelings ravaging her, and the music did its best to oblige, but it wasn't enough. Every beat of every song, she could feel his eyes on her. With every wriggle of her hips and every wave of her hands in the air came a fight not to turn around and seek him out. So desperately in tune was she to him that the whump of her heart told her of his approach long before her head whipped around to confirm it.

He'd removed his dinner jacket and bow tie. Undone the top two buttons of his shirt.

She tried to pretend his appearance on the dance floor meant nothing, she really tried, but she could no more stop her eyes from finding his than she could stop the beats of her ragged heart. Could no more stop her body gravitating to him than she could stop her lungs from working. Could no more stop the flames from flickering low in her abdomen at the sight of his chest hair where his shirt had opened than she could stop her name being Gabrielle Jeanne Breton.

As in the banquet, the world around them seemed to disintegrate. The ravishing blonde who Gabrielle had been dancing beside and who'd made sure Gabrielle, the outsider, was kept within their group and included in the funky dance moves she led, became blurred.

Gaze intent on her, snake hips swaying, he rested a hand loosely on her hip. His other hand captured hers. Or did her hand capture his?

A new track came on.

Eyes fused, they began to move.

The party continued around them, periphery extras in their private dance for two.

The ache in her feet had disappeared. If she didn't have Andrés anchoring her to the dance floor she felt she might have floated to the ceiling.

Another track played. Slower in tempo. Much slower.

They slowed down with it.

The hand at her hip slid around her waist and pulled her closer.

Andrés blew the stale air in his lungs out slowly. The weighty beats of his heart rippled through his entire being.

His shirt acted as the barrier between the skin on his back and Gabrielle's hand but he could feel the burn of her touch as strongly as if he were naked. He kept catching wafts of the delightful scents that had tantalised him throughout the banquet. The urge to bury his nose into the top of her head and inhale her shampoo deeply into his lungs was becoming torture to deny himself.

The deep thrums of awareness zinging through his veins and over his skin were growing too, increasing with every sway to the music.

The flickers of arousal were fighting to burn into flames.

He needed to do something to distract him from the effects of the sexy creature he was dancing with before he lost the fight. The sensible thing would be to remove himself from the situation, leave the dance floor and give himself a few moments for the arousal to simmer back to a manageable level.

Andrés had never chosen the sensible option in his life.

'How are you enjoying the party?' he murmured.

'Very well, thank you.' She answered with such politeness that he moved his head back a little so he could look down at her face. The Gabrielle Breton who'd been at his side the entire evening had been many things towards him but polite was not one of them. He didn't count her efforts at politeness when she'd searched his car as the underlying bite had negated it. Her lack of deference was one of the many things he liked about her.

Oh, yes, he liked this woman, and not just because he found her the sexiest creature to walk this earth. He liked her humour. Liked her intelligence. Liked her compassion. Liked her commitment. Liked her straight talking. Liked her enthusiasm for food. Liked the pulse in her eyes whenever their gazes locked together. Liked that when he'd snaked his way to her on the dance floor she'd looked at him as if he were the only man in the world.

She was holding herself stiffly, her gaze fixed over his shoulder making it impossible to read her expression.

'Glad you came?'

'Yes,' she replied with the same politeness. 'Thank you for inviting me.'

'It has been my pleasure.'

Another slow song began to play.

The crowd around them continued to mush-room. The floor space they had to call their own continued to shrink, forcing their bodies even closer.

The swell of her breasts crushed into his chest. A rush of awareness strong enough to fell a horse thickened his loins. If they hadn't been so closely entwined he would have missed the hitch of Gabrielle's breath, missed the shud-der that ran the length of her body, missed the almost imperceptible tightening of her fingers on his back.

'I mean it,' he murmured, finally giving into temptation and rubbing his nose into her hair. The strands felt like silk. 'Having you as my date has been a delight, Gabrielle.'

Dios, this woman *did* something to him.

Gabrielle's head was still spinning with the blood that had rushed to it at the first crush of their bodies. Pressed so tightly against the hard-ness of Andrés's torso, his breaths dancing into the roots of her hair, the musky heat of his skin and cologne dancing in her airwaves and their bodies swaying in time together, it was all she could do to keep her legs upright, never mind push him away so she could run.

Because she should run. This was madness. Dancing with him like this was madness. She was feeding the ravenous butterflies in her belly and stoking the flames of a desire that could never be given air.

But her body was begging her to press even closer. Her breasts were as sensitised as she'd ever imagined they could be and pleading to be crushed tighter into his chest, the skin on her back aching to feel the hand making slow circular motions against it without the barrier of her dress.

That same hand moved lower to caress her bottom.

Impulse overcame reason and she turned her face to the opened part of his shirt and rubbed her nose against his exposed throat and breathed him in.

The musk of Andrés's cologne and another underlying scent…the scent of his skin…filled her airwaves at the same moment she became aware of the hardness pressing against her abdomen. The thrill that rushed through her was so strong it knocked the air from her lungs and infected every cell in her body with pulsing heat. For one heady, tantalising moment she ground herself into the hardness only to come to her senses with a shock that had her yanking herself out of his arms.

Her cheeks burning at her own wantonness, she met his hooded stare and somehow managed to speak through the raggedness of her breaths. 'I need air.'

Terrified to look at him a moment longer, Gabrielle span around and slipped her way through the pulsing dance floor to escape.

Andrés watched Gabrielle disappear into the crowd with his heart thumping wildly.

Dios, he could hardly breathe through the desire blazing through him, but he filled his lungs and then, uncaring of the dancing couples he had to push out of his way, set off after her.

He'd just cleared the dance floor when she vanished through the opened French doors that led out into the palace gardens.

Following her lead, he stepped out into the quieter, warm sweet air.

Only a handful of other people were out there, sitting on the benches of the perimeter patio… and then he spotted her in the distance, shoes in hand, treading over the immaculate lawn to the nineteenth century gazebo that looked like a miniature castle in its own right, her path lit by tiny nightlights and the stars high in the night sky twinkling down on her.

He descended the steps and stepped onto the grass.

His stride being twice the length of hers, he made an effort to slow his pace and give her a little of the space she needed.

He was closing in on her when she sank onto one of the marble benches. He was out of her eye line but she must have sensed his approach for she turned her face to him before he'd put his foot onto the first of the gazebo's steps.

She'd done the same on the dance floor he remembered. Sensed his approach.

Propping himself against a pillar a good distance from her, Andrés studied her without speaking. Just as she'd sensed his approach, he sensed that he should wait until Gabrielle was ready to break the silence.

It felt like it took for ever before her quiet voice cut through the still night. 'I'm sorry for running out on you like that.'

'I frightened you?'

She swallowed and then shook her head slowly. 'I frightened myself. Andrés…' Her voice caught but she didn't drop her stare from his. 'This isn't *me*. I don't… I don't do this.'

He didn't need her to explain what *this* was. They were both adults. Adults sharing the strongest chemistry it was possible to be caught in.

He took a deep breath, hating to vocalise the question he knew he must ask. 'Do you want me to get my driver to take you home?'

Gabrielle got to her feet and took a step towards him before she even realised what she was doing.

Until he'd asked the question she would have said yes: take me home. She'd escaped into the palace gardens to cool her overheated body and get air that was fresh enough to clear her mind enough to think rationally into her lungs.

Except no matter how rationally she tried to think, the only thing to race around in her mind was how thrilling it had felt to be crushed against Andrés…and how badly she longed to be crushed against him again. Not just to be crushed against him but to bury her face in his strong throat and feel the warmth of his skin against her and refill her lungs with his scent and experience the pleasure of his hands caressing her in all the places she'd never been touched.

She drifted closer and gazed up at him.

His jaw was clenched, magnificent body tensed.

Without the extra inches the shoes gave her, he seemed even taller and broader. Even more virile.

She leaned her face closer to his, closer to the magnetic darkness of Andrés's black eyes and unthinkingly lifted a hand to touch his face.

Moving with a stealth-like grace no man of his size should possess, he caught her hand mid-air and snatched the other too, holding them firmly as he brought his face even closer to hers.

Gabrielle could feel herself falling into the

hypnotic swirl, couldn't have broken the lock of their gazes if she tried… Didn't *want* to break the lock.

Releasing a hand to grip her hip and maintain the few inches of air separating their bodies, he pressed the tip of his nose to hers. 'Do you want my driver to take you home?' he repeated hoarsely. 'If you want to leave then all you have to do is say. I will step away from you and call my driver to collect you and see you safely back to your apartment.' His breathing became heavier, each word whispering against the delicate skin of her sensitised lips. 'What do you say, Gabrielle? Do you want me to make that call?'

The alternative went unspoken. Nothing more needed to be said.

Skimming her fingers up his arm, she placed her palm on his chest. He sucked in a breath. His grip on her hip tightened. The thuds of his heartbeat perfectly matched the thuds of her own.

In a brief moment of clarity she realised that the alternative wouldn't mean breaking the promise she'd made to herself when she'd brought Lucas home. Andrés was a strictly short-term relationship man. He wouldn't want more than she could give, and all she could give him was one night. It was all she could give to herself.

This was meant to be, she realised, staring even deeper into his eyes. It had been from the start. If she'd known he was single, she would have refused point blank to attend the party with him, would have spent the night alone in her tiny apartment unaware that he held the key to unlocking all the desires she'd kept buried so deep for Lucas's sake that she'd hardly been aware they existed.

For this one night she could put those desires first, and do so with the sexiest man to roam the earth, the man who had the power to turn her to liquid without even touching her.

A man who wouldn't want anything more from her.

She moved her face closer. Their lips brushed like feathers. The heat of his breath filled her senses.

The butterflies in her belly had grown so big the beat of their wings had become at one with the beats of her heart. She was barely aware of her hand sliding up from his chest to cup the back of his strong neck, not until she felt the scorch of their flesh connecting. The thrill of Andrés's fingers biting deeper into her hips sent a tiny moan escaping in the moment their mouths fused together, and then she was caught in a kiss so deep and sensuous that the last thought before she lost the last of her mind was that Andrés's kisses tasted of hedonistic heaven.

Nerve endings on fire, Gabrielle dug the

tips of her fingers through the soft bristles of his hair, and melted into the most passionate and thrilling moment of her entire life. The first slide of his tongue against her own sent a fireball of desire screaming through her, and she held onto him tightly as the dance of their mouths deepened into a hunger that had every cell in her body begging for more.

Laughter close by echoed in the night air and penetrated the sensual vortex Andrés had fallen into.

With a muttered curse, he broke away from the woman who, with one hungry kiss, had fully aroused him in a way he'd never experienced before.

This went bone deep. Marrow deep. Hunger fuelling hunger.

The feel of those pillowy lips against his and that sweet tongue in his mouth…

Smothering a groan, he took a step away from the temptation that was Gabrielle, muttered another curse and dragged air into his lungs.

What the hell was he doing?

They were in the Monte Cleure palace garden. Anyone could see them. He needed to get control of himself.

Another lungful of air and he let himself look at Gabrielle.

The expression on her dazed face perfectly matched the torture he was experiencing.

He'd never known lust could grip so swiftly. So completely.

With another groan, he closed the gap he'd only just created and hooked an arm around her waist.

'You never answered my question,' he said, his words harsher than he'd intended. The depth of the attraction between them was a life-force of its own but he would not take advantage of her if any trace of the doubts and fears that had seen her run from the ball room still existed.

Her gaze locked onto his. A hand flew to his chest. Fingers pinched at the silk of his shirt. Her breasts were rising and falling in rapid motion.

He found himself holding his breath as he waited for her to respond.

The pillowy lips parted. 'I don't want to leave without you.'

Still gazing into her desire-filled dark brown depths, he breathed in deeply, his relief at her softly delivered words close to overwhelming.

What magic ran in Gabrielle's veins? he wondered. Her beauty grew every time he looked at her but the world was overrun with beautiful women. If he was being dispassionate, he would say there was nothing special about her. No goodly reason on earth that one kiss with her, one simple connection of their mouths, the aperitif of courtship, should blow his mind so badly.

No goodly reason that he felt he would combust if he didn't get one more taste of that potent magic.

But then her pillowy lips parted again and closed in on his, and he realised dispassion had already gone to hell when it came to this woman.

Their lips melded together for one long, lingering kiss that roused his senses completely.

Breaking the kiss, he gripped the hand still locked against his chest and rubbed his nose into her soft cheek. 'Let's get out of here.'

Detouring only to collect Gabrielle's bag and Andrés's dinner jacket and bowtie, they slipped out of the palace, hands clasped together, without saying goodbye to anyone. It was a rudeness that wouldn't go unnoticed but Andrés didn't care. Let them say what they wanted. They could add it to the rudeness he'd displayed when he'd given his entire attention to Gabrielle during the banquet.

He took a deep breath. It had been many years since his guts had been filled with such nerves and excitement.

His driver crunched his car over the palace courtyard. By unspoken agreement, they were going to Andrés's apartment.

In the back of the car, he took a moment to breathe before looking again at Gabrielle.

Her wide-eyed stare was already fixed on him, her body twisted to face him. The silence was so total he could hear the shallowness of her breaths.

Dios, he'd never known his heart could beat so hard.

Without speaking, he pressed the button that darkened the dividing glass, giving them complete privacy. Only dim lights illuminated them.

He leaned closer to her and put a hand on her thigh. She visibly trembled.

Eyes locked on hers, he slowly, slowly gathered the velvet of her dress up to her trembling knee.

'It has been a long time since you were with a man?' he guessed quietly, splaying his hand over the soft skin of her naked thigh. It took all his control not to grip it tightly.

Something he couldn't read flickered in her eyes before she nodded.

He brought his face closer to hers. He had to swallow the moisture that had filled his mouth to speak again. 'We don't have to do anything you don't want. We don't have to do anything at all.' Although if he never got another taste of those beautiful pillowy lips he had a feeling a part of him might just well die...

Instead of saying anything, she palmed his jaw. The pads of her fingers dug into his cheek as she brought her mouth to his for a feather-light caress.

She pulled away to look into his eyes again before bringing her lips back to his for a harder, more substantial kiss and then, with the softest moan, her lips parted, her tongue danced into his mouth and the spark caught.

Mouths locked, they devoured each other. Every sweep of Gabrielle's tongue against his sent fire to his loins and fed the hunger…fed it but left him ravenous.

Laying her down so she was flat on her back, the velvet skirt of her dress bunched around her hips, one knee raised, a bare foot pressed against his thigh, the other trailing on the car floor, he dragged his fingers over the most succulent thigh imaginable. The mew of arousal that sounded from her throat fed his own rock-hard arousal. Covering her with his body, he kissed her again.

A vague awareness that they would arrive at his apartment shortly echoed in the back of his head, and he broke the lock of their mouths for another look at the beauty that captivated him more with every stare.

She lifted her hand to run her fingers through his hair. The desire blazing on her face was like nothing he'd seen before. It was there in the slash of colour high on her cheeks and the heavy-lidded, drugged dilation in her eyes.

One more taste, he promised himself. Just one more taste and then he would help her sit up, straighten the skirt of her dress, and control his ardour until they reached his apartment.

Maybe he would have been able to make good on his mental promise of just *one more taste* if, when he crushed his mouth back to hers, his fingers hadn't crept further up her thigh and clasped onto a bottom so plump and peachy that every cell in his body shot to electrified attention.

It was possible that he would still have been able to break away if she hadn't raised her pelvis and, with another of those soft mews, hooked her leg around him.

Keeping their mouths fused together, Andrés lifted himself slightly, giving just the space needed to bring his hand around to Gabrielle's pelvis. He cupped it whole. *Dios*, the *heat*...

The moment Andrés put his hand to her pubis, Gabrielle lost the last of any inhibitions she had left. With one touch, the ache that had been slowly growing as the evening had gone on turned into an acute delicious pain begging for something, *something*. Moaning into his mouth, she twisted her body so both her legs wrapped around him, and ground into his hand. When his fingers dipped under her knickers and cupped her without any barrier, the sensations were so good and so powerful that all she could do was rock into his hand in the urgent need for that something. She was barely conscious of fighting with the button and zip of his trousers until his giant hand abandoned the source of her pleasure to cover hers and free his arousal.

She sucked in a breath as he curled her fingers over the pulsing hot length before his hand dove back between her legs, aware only that Andrés's grunts as she gripped his erection and made the movements that turned his grunts into groans were as exciting and thrilling as what his hand was doing to her.

Groans turned into shallow breaths, their mouths touching but hardly moving. The urgency for that *something* grew, and she gazed into his glazed eyes, silently pleading with him to…

He shifted the angle of his hand so a finger slid inside her sticky heat and his palm cupped harder to her pubis. She gasped at the pleasure and reflexively tightened her grip on his erection as she ground against his palm and then she felt it, the release of the coil that had wound tighter and tighter inside her and spasm after spasm of the most intense pleasure imaginable flooded her and turned the world around her into flickering white light.

CHAPTER SEVEN

IT WAS ONLY the beauty of Gabrielle's face lighting up in shocked wonder as she lost control that stopped Andrés giving in to his own release. It caught him in his own shocked wonder.

He'd come so close. So damn close.

When she had finally stilled and the only movement was in the dazed eyes ringing at him, he inhaled deeply to bring about the final bit of control needed, and kissed her gently.

He thought Gabrielle's climax might just be the most beautiful and erotic thing he had ever witnessed.

Somehow managing to trap his erection in the tight confines of his underwear, he pulled the zip of his trousers up as light filtered through the car's tinted windows.

'We are here,' he told her huskily.

She blinked, raised her head and then let it flop back onto the seat. Her chest rose as she took a long breath.

'Are you okay?' he asked, lightly tracing the back of his finger over her cheek.

Her pillowy lips attempted a smile. 'A bit shaky.'

He shifted to free Gabrielle's leg trapped between him and the car seat. 'Good shaky or bad shaky?'

Her next smile was a little more convincing and came with a short laugh. 'Good shaky...' She pressed her thighs together and twisted so both her feet dropped to the floor. 'I think.'

'Do you need me to carry you inside?' he half jested.

This time, her smile pulled across her whole face. 'What, like a *real* princess?'

He couldn't explain why this touched him as it did, but he had to fight to keep the lightness in his tone. 'Just like a real princess.'

The car came to a stop.

She held a hand out. 'I think I'm good to walk but I could do with your help sitting up.'

He took hold of it and grazed a kiss to the tip of her fingers then pulled her upright.

Between them, they tugged the skirt of her dress back down to her ankles—pretty ankles, he noted—before Andrés slid her shoes back onto her feet.

'Now I am a real princess,' Gabrielle teased as the door opened.

Only when he turned his back to her so he could unfold himself out was she able to take the moment to properly compose herself without his watchful stare on her before swinging her legs out of the car, taking Andrés's hand

and joining him in the Imperium's private underground car park.

If he didn't have such tight hold of her hand she thought it possible her shaky legs really would have given way.

She had never imagined...never *dreamed*... that pleasure could be so intense. That a climax could leave you feeling like your bones had melted.

And if she'd thought about it, she wouldn't have dreamed that she could behave in such a wanton way and not feel an ounce of shame... but that was part of the Andrés effect, she realised. It wasn't just that he wore his sexuality like a second skin but the look that pulsed in his hypnotic eyes, the sense that this was a man who embraced all the sensual pleasures life had to offer...and as she thought this, the spent flame deep in her pelvis flickered back to life at the sensual discoveries that lay ahead of her.

She wished she could tell him that she'd just experienced her first ever climax but feared it would lead to a conversation she mustn't have. She'd already proven herself incapable of lying to him and...

Oh, just stop thinking!

Stepping into the elevator Andrés guided her to, she met his stare as the doors closed around them.

To think they hadn't even made it into his apartment yet…

A burst of laughter came from nowhere, and she wrapped her arms around his waist and gazed up at Andrés's devastatingly handsome face.

He squeezed her bottom. 'Are you going to share the joke?'

'There is no joke. I just felt like laughing.' Gabrielle lifted herself onto her toes and kissed him.

No point in analysing what had just happened to her. She'd made the choice to embrace the Andrés effect and it was more potent than she could have dreamed, but just as with everything else that had happened to her that evening, come the morning the magic would go pop and she would return to her real life. Nothing like this would ever happen to her again.

No point either, in worrying that she was already finding Andrés's kisses headily addictive.

The elevator door slid open.

She hadn't even felt it move.

Happily slipping her hand into his, she stepped into a different welcome room to the one she'd arrived at via the atrium and as a far more elaborate door to the other welcome room swung open, an unexpected thought made her heart lurch and rooted her feet to the floor.

'What's wrong?' Andrés asked.

'Sophia.' Gabrielle didn't think she could look the Spanish woman in the eye. It was one thing approving—*suggesting*—a border guard accompany her brother to a party as a last-minute substitute, quite another for the brother to bring that same border guard home.

He coaxed her over the threshold. 'You have nothing to worry about. She's flown back to Seville.'

A man who looked to be around the fifty mark and who was wearing a monogrammed black polo shirt with *AM* embroidered into it materialised. Andrés acknowledged him with a nod then held his arms back so the man could remove his dinner jacket for him, all the while continuing their conversation, saying, 'She messaged earlier. Said she was bored being stuck in the apartment on her own and wanted to sleep in her own bed. Thank you, Michael,' he added in English to the man Gabrielle assumed was some kind of butler. 'You can finish for the evening now.'

The man bowed his head. 'Goodnight, sir.'

'Goodnight, Michael.'

As if by magic, the man disappeared as unobtrusively as he'd appeared, although Gabrielle thought she might have had a better idea of the direction he'd taken if her stare hadn't been glued to Andrés.

Suddenly she felt very much aware that it was only the two of them and for the first time experienced a frisson of nerves, nerves that increased when he took her hand and led her through a different door to the one she'd taken earlier. It was a kitchen. A kitchen so startling in its contrast to her own tiny cooking space that all she could do was shake her head in awe.

'Champagne?' Andrés asked.

'Sure you can manage without your butler to do it for you?' she teased.

That was better. He'd sensed the stillness of his apartment working to feed Gabrielle's nerves. Her teasing already felt familiar. Felt good.

'I'm sure I can work it out,' he said with wry self-deprecation, then opened the fridge. This one was full of food. Closing it, he opened the adjacent one and was greeted with rows and rows of white wine, rosé and champagne. Selecting a bottle of Louis Roederer, he opened cupboards in the search of champagne flutes.

'You don't know your way around your own kitchen?' she said with a splutter of laughter as he opened the third cupboard.

He grinned sheepishly. 'I keep spirits and glasses in the bar in the living room that I help myself to whenever the mood takes me. That is the extent of my domesticity. I'm afraid I wasn't exaggerating the lengths I go to avoid chores.'

'Is champagne a Michael job?'

'It isn't an Andrés job.'

She arched an unimpressed eyebrow. 'If you refer to yourself in the third person again, I'm going home.'

'Andrés would never refer to himself in the third person.'

Feeling ridiculously pleased at Gabrielle's sniggers at this, he opened the door that led into a pantry and found a shelf full of crystal champagne flutes.

He was even more ridiculously pleased to return to the kitchen and find Gabrielle had hoisted herself onto the marble island and kicked her shoes off.

With a wink, he worked the cork and in one quick move, it popped.

'Hidden talents. I'm impressed.' She laughed.

He blew her a kiss then poured them both a glass. When he handed Gabrielle her flute, he kissed her for real, a short, hard, hungry kiss that flooded him with heat.

Dios, what was she doing to him?

Who the hell cared? Tonight was turning into the best night of his life and he wasn't prepared to waste another minute of it by thinking.

He raised his flute. *'Salud.'*

'Santé.'

Flutes clinked together, they drank.

Champagne fizzing on his tongue, Andrés stood before her and drank the whole of her in. With the bright kitchen lights bathing her, he would expect to find the imperfections that the clever lighting of the palace shadowed, but all he found was her beauty enhanced. She was breathtaking.

He traced the pads of his fingers over her cheek. *'Tu es belle,'* he murmured.

Her chest rose slowly and then she expelled the breath with a sigh of pleasure. 'I didn't know you spoke my language.'

He hovered his hand. *'Un peu.'* A little. His chest swelling, he drank her beauty in some more then plucked the flute from her hold and placed it with his own on the island before putting his hands to her slim waist. 'Let's share a bath.'

Her eyes widened but she didn't object.

He pressed a light kiss to her irresistible lips and whispered, 'I am not in any rush, *ma belle.* Let's make the whole night count.'

Despite the heated arousal that had infected every cell of his body, Andrés wanted to make the most of every minute he had with this

woman. He wanted to know her intimately...
In every possible way.

Gabrielle experienced a moment of weight-lessness as she was lifted off the island. Once her feet were on the ground, Andrés moved his hands from her waist, expertly picked up their flutes with one hand and reached for the champagne bottle with the other.

His eyes gleamed as he beckoned for her to follow him.

She allowed herself only a moment's hesitation before making her feet move.

She wasn't actually sure why she hadn't just said no to the suggestion of sharing a bath. She'd had the opportunity. A fear of seeming gauche and unsophisticated? No, it couldn't be that. He already knew she didn't have a sophisticated bone in her body.

She could still say no. Tell him the truth.

But how could she admit that she was terri-fied as she'd never been naked in front of a man before? She couldn't. As with her never having climaxed before, it would only lead to questions she couldn't answer.

But she wished she could. Wished she could tell him the truth about everything...

Stop thinking, Gabrielle!

Yes. Stop thinking. She'd known the night would involve them taking all their clothes off but she'd assumed it would be in a bedroom with the lights out.

Oh, help, what if her naked body turned him off? Could that happen?

Oh, shut up, brain!

Falling into step beside him, she finally quietened her brain and treaded over carpet her bare feet practically cried with joy to be walking on.

He pushed a door open with his elbow and Gabrielle found herself in a bathroom of such size and opulence that her mouth fell open.

And she'd thought the bathroom she'd showered in earlier was amazing.

Stepping over the colourful mosaic floor, she slowly took in the clean white tiles of the high walls and the embellished gold architrave, and then her gaze drifted back down to the enormous walk-in shower—twice the size at least of the one she'd showered in earlier—at the far end before finally resting on the long, sunken bath.

The lights dimmed, bathing the entire room in a romantic golden hue.

She snatched a breath before allowing her gaze to fall on Andrés.

He was watching her with an expression that set her heart pounding all over again.

'Do you need to call Michael to show you how to work the bath?' she said teasingly, needing to break the silence she knew her own nerves had created.

He stared pointedly at her before turning to a keypad built into the wall and pressing a button on it. Less than a second later and streaming water gushed out of dozens of hidden internal faucets. Next, he poured a liberal amount of bubble bath into it and immediately the most mouth-watering scent filled the air.

'See?' he said, his tone serious. 'Andrés can run a bath.'

Mirth bubbled up in her in the same way the bubbles foaming in the bath were rising. 'Very impressive,' she said with a snigger.

Smirking, he dropped a wink. 'I like to think so.' Then, without missing a beat, his fingers went to the buttons of his shirt. In moments, he'd shrugged it off. He let it drop to the floor and moved his hand to the button of his trousers.

Gabrielle's mouth ran dry. She'd caught a glimpse of his naked chest when she'd first arrived at his apartment, had touched the contours of it over his shirt but even so…

Nothing could have prepared her for the raw beauty of it. Every inch, from the deep olive hue of his skin to the dark hair that covered from the band of his trousers up over the washboard stomach and smattered over his defined pecs… beautiful. And his *arms*… They were a work of art in their own right, even without the sexy sleeve tattoo.

He watched her ogling and grinned. 'You like what you see?'

She tried to affect nonchalance. 'It's…quite pleasing.'

His eyes glittered knowingly. In one fell swoop, he pulled his trousers and underwear down and stepped out of them, taking his black socks with them.

The mouth that had become so arid the Sahara would have felt sorry for it suddenly flooded with moisture.

Fully, unashamedly naked, Andrés's body transcended beauty. This was masculinity in its purest form, a feat even Michelangelo would have struggled to replicate even when considering he'd have had to greatly reduce the size of a certain aroused appendage so as not to fall foul of obscenity laws, and it came to her in a flash why she hadn't objected to sharing a bath with him.

The thought was too thrilling to refuse.

He stepped to her.

Her abdomen contracted.

'Turn around,' he ordered huskily.

Legs suddenly trembling again, she obeyed.

Warm hands clasped her arms. Warm breath

danced into her hair. His erection jutted into her back. 'Lift your arms.'

Closing her eyes, resisting the strong yearning to lean back into him, she again obeyed.

He pinched the tiny hidden zipper that ran beneath her armpit and tugged it down slowly all the way to where it met the skirt of her dress. Then he brought his hand to her shoulder and pinched the dress where it swept over it, and brushed it down her arm. The top part of her dress folded in a swoop to her waist, exposing her naked breasts.

Her whole body was trembling.

Giant hands cupped her breasts.

She could no longer stop herself from swaying back into him. His fingers gently squeezed, capturing her nipples.

The sensations were so intense that she moaned and arched her back, pushing her chest forwards in a wordless plea for more.

His breathing deepened and he groaned into her hair. '*Tu es si belle*, Gabrielle. So beautiful.'

She could have wept when his hands abandoned her breasts to palm gently over her stomach to where her dress had fallen to. Still breathing heavily into her hair, he found the clasp at her waist. There was a rip as he grew impatient at the fiddliness of it and tore at it, and then heavy velvet pooled at her feet.

His erection now a thick rock pressed into her

back, he pinched the sides of her panties and tugged them down her hips. A sudden impatience to be as naked as him had Gabrielle take over and wiggle them down her legs and kick them off.

His hand caught hold of hers and twisted her to face him.

The look on his face would have blown away any of the shyness she'd expected to feel at being naked in front of a man for the first time. But there hadn't been any shyness since he'd taken her breasts in his hands and held them so reverentially. Only arousal. An arousal that deepened at the hooded hunger in his stare.

Impulse had her close her lips around a flat, brown nipple. He groaned and clasped her bottom, pulling her flush against him. His arousal stabbed into her belly and before she could even think about what she was doing, she dropped to her knees and kissed the tip.

Andrés could hardly draw breath. His feet were ground to the floor, refusing to cooperate with his brain's command to step back, to reset things to the slow seduction he'd…

She took him in her mouth.

Holy…

She drew her lips back slowly then, keeping his length clasped in her hand, looked up at him with those deeply beautiful eyes and, almost shyly said, 'Do you like this?'

He had to swallow to speak. 'Yes, but, Gabrielle...'

His intention to tell her to stop, that he was already too close to the edge, dissolved when those pillowy lips enclosed around him again.

Holy, holy...

With a growl, he clasped her head with all the gentleness he could muster, withdrew from her mouth, then reached down, scooped hold of her waist and lifted her into his arms.

Then, without a word, he carried her to his bedroom and practically threw her onto the bed.

Gabrielle gazed at the man roughly parting her thighs and dazedly thought, *I've caused this. I've done this to him.*

Just as he was to blame for turning her entire body into a molten pool of hot, sticky desire, she was to blame for the pulsing black eyes and aroused tension etched on his face.

His erection jutting against her pubis, he snatched her hands and pressed them either side of her head.

Breathing heavily, jaw clenched, he gazed down at her.

'Kiss me,' she breathed.

He closed his eyes tightly and then they locked back onto hers. And then his mouth swooped for a kiss so savage in its passion that at the first fusion of their lips, Gabrielle found herself lost in the sensation that was Andrés, and it was the most incredible sensation in the world.

There was something almost unleashed in his kisses and the graze of his tongue as he touched and tasted every inch of her, a sense that he wanted to bite his way through her skin and burrow himself inside.

This was Andrés stripped back to his animalistic, masculine essence and it was the most hedonistic, mind-blowing pleasure imaginable.

Every suck and caress of her breasts added to the exquisite agony. Every drag of his fingers over her thighs and belly stoked the fire, releasing the animalistic feminine essence she hadn't even guessed lived inside her. When he buried his face between her legs, she grabbed his hair and urged him on, begging and pleading until her second climax ripped through her and her pleas became cries of bliss.

This time though, there was no time to luxuriate in the sensations because the spasms had hardly abated when his giant body covered her and his mouth connected with hers for another bone-melting kiss. With his arousal pressed against her pleading folds, she instinctively spread her thighs further apart and raised her pelvis.

She gasped at the first push of his arousal inside her heat.

This was it, she thought wildly. *The point of no return.*

She had never wanted anything more in the whole of her life.

'Protection,' he groaned, even as he pushed a little deeper. 'We need…'

Swearing, he pulled out of her, stretched out an arm and yanked his bedside drawer open.

Gabrielle barely had the time to be grateful for Andrés finding sense for them both when he'd sheathed himself and he was back exactly where she wanted him to be.

With one hand clenched in hers, the other gripping her hip, with one long thrust he buried himself deep inside her.

The shock made Gabrielle suck in a breath and freeze.

Had that been *pain*?

Andrés had stopped moving. She could feel the thumps of his heart against her breast. Had it hurt him too…? But then he pulled back almost to the tip and with a groan of what could only be pleasure, drove back inside her.

Oh, that was better. Much better.

He lifted his head and kissed her.

By the fourth thrust, she'd adjusted to the newness and the sensation of being completely filled.

By the sixth thrust she'd stopped counting.

Arms and legs wrapped tightly around him, she closed her eyes and submitted to the burning flames of the passion scorching them both.

Andrés would never have believed something could feel so good. So damn incredible.

Incredible.

Dios, she was so *tight*…

Release hung tantalisingly close but he wanted to make this last as long as he could and experience every one of Gabrielle's soft cries of pleasure, to feel her nails dig into his skin, to be inside her as one with her…

Her hold on him tightened, her moans deepening, and he sensed her climax building.

Needing to watch, he placed a lingering kiss to her lips then raised himself onto his elbows, adjusting the lock of their groins to increase the friction she needed.

With drugged-like movements, her head moved from side to side, pillowy lips parting, colour rising on her cheeks and then she was clinging to him, her back arching and then her eyes flew open and he felt the most powerful thickening around him, pulling him deeper and deeper until he could hold on no more and the pleasure of release saturated him in vivid, powerful colour.

CHAPTER EIGHT

IT WAS FOUR A.M. and they'd finally made it to the bath.

After making love a second time, the water had gone cold so Andrés had run them a fresh one and lit candles so their only illumination was the soft romantic glow of candlelight. It suited Gabrielle's mood completely.

Sipping at yet another flute of champagne—they were on their second bottle—she gazed at the gorgeous face of the man who had taken her to such dizzying heights and sighed.

His foot pressed against her hip. Both of them were stretched out, facing each other, legs entwined. 'Are you okay?'

She smiled at his concern. 'Very okay, thank you. Just thinking I don't want this night to end.' Then, in case he thought she was suggesting something, added, 'Real life awaits me, but it isn't here yet so let's just enjoy the time we have left and I'll try to catch up on sleep before Maman and Romeo bring Lucas back.'

The face he pulled made her smile widen. '*Romeo?* Your brother is called *Romeo*?'

She giggled softly. 'I know. I told you, my mother's a reader. She went through a Shakespeare phase when she was pregnant with him.'

'What phase was she going through when she was pregnant with you?'

Her giggle turned into a snigger. 'I have no idea—my dad had put his foot down by the time I was born and insisted on normal names.'

'You are one of how many?'

'Three,' she replied, glad he'd phrased the question in a way that meant her answer wouldn't turn the conversation onto darker territory. 'I'm the youngest.'

'The baby of the family like me.'

She prodded his thigh with her toe. 'I bet you hated being the baby.'

Andrés breathed through the tightening of his chest. He'd never known anyone to get him the way Gabrielle instinctively seemed to. If he didn't know better he would think she had a conduit to his brain. 'Loathed it,' he admitted.

Her teeth flashed. 'Knew it.'

'How?'

She shrugged. One of her breasts crested above the inches-deep bath foam, giving him a tantalising glimpse of its succulent perfection. 'I don't know. I just can't imagine you being happy being coddled and petted and told you were too young to do the things your big sister was allowed to do.'

'When I was small, my grandmother always used to pinch my cheek when she visited and tell me what a cute little boy I was.' He grunted at the memory. 'I hated being babied. The worst was when Sophia was old enough to be left in charge of me. She took an evil delight in bossing me around.'

'Did you put up with it?'

'What do you think?'

Her eyes narrowed in contemplation. 'I think you probably took an evil delight in winding her up.'

He grinned at her astuteness. 'And you? No, let me guess…' Narrowing his own eyes in contemplation, he said, 'No one babied you.'

Her eyes flashed with surprise. 'How did you guess?'

'You haven't got a spoilt bone in your body.' And what a body it was, he thought, his loins stirring just to remember what lay beneath the thick bath foam.

The dress Gabrielle had worn that night had displayed her curves to perfection but he'd been prepared for the signs of birth. They would have made no difference to him—to Andrés, the stretchmarks of the belly and thighs, and the loosening of the flesh of the breasts that came with birth should be worn as a badge of honour for the giving of life—but Gabrielle had none of them. Her breasts were plump and succulent, her belly and thighs toned, not even a silvery sliver of a stretchmark on them.

Had her young age when having her son protected her from those effects? he wondered. He was no expert, had only a vague memory of his mother's stretch-marked body from the days she'd sunbathed in a bikini in their tiny garden when he'd been growing up to go on, so what did he know?

Still, it was strange. Surely childbirth should leave some form of mark on the body?

'Romeo's five years older than me and was always too busy knocking a ball about with his friends to pay much attention to me,' she said, breaking through his thoughts. 'He's always looked out for me though.'

'He looks out for your son?'

'As much as he can. He works on an oil rig, six weeks on, two weeks off. His girlfriend lives in Cadiz so when he's off he splits his time between us and her.'

'And your other… You never said if it was a brother or sister.'

Sadness flitted over her face and she looked away, draining her champagne before answering. 'A sister. Eloise. If I'd been born a week earlier we would have been in the same school year.'

'I went to school with identical twins born

four minutes apart. Sergio told everyone who would listen that he was the eldest.'

She smiled at the anecdote but the sadness remained. 'Eloise was never like that.'

By the time Gabrielle started school, she'd already known in the instinctive way that children just knew things that Eloise needed protecting.

'Enough talk,' she declared.

A thick black eyebrow rose. 'Oh?'

Tonight was the first night Gabrielle had taken for herself since bringing Lucas home, a memory she knew she would treasure for the rest of her life. To bring Eloise into it when just saying her name made her heart weep…

Foam clinging to parts of her, she got to her knees and sloshed through the water to straddle Andrés's lap. Emptying the last of the second champagne bottle into their flutes, she clinked hers to his and drank it in one go. Aroused amusement on his face, Andrés followed suit.

Both flutes empty, she placed them next to the empty bottles on the low fitted cupboard that ran behind where his head rested, then placed her hands on his chest and leaned her face down to his.

She was drunk she realised, drunk on alcohol and drunk on Andrés.

Holding his cheeks, she kissed him deeply, and welcomed the glorious sensations that roared to life with the fusion of their mouths and tongues, sensations strong enough to drive out all thought and give them the moment for what it was. Pleasure.

For the first time Gabrielle really understood what she'd committed to missing when she'd committed herself to a lifetime of celibacy.

Intimacy and pleasure. All the things most people her age took for granted.

And emotional connection.

It was the latter she suspected she would feel the most bereft to leave when she walked out of this apartment.

Whether the desire consuming her would have sparked to life with anyone else was pointless in trying to guess, but she knew in her heart that the magical alchemy that had enveloped them so completely was a one-off, and she would take every ounce of the pleasure and connection they could share with each other until the time came to say goodbye, because she would never have any of this again.

That time was speeding towards them.

Dragging her mouth over the bristles of Andrés's beard, she slipped her fingers around his head to clasp his skull and lifted herself so he could take a breast into his mouth.

Hands trailing up and down her spine, his hungry mouth and tongue working their magic,

Gabrielle threw her head back and lost herself to the heady sensations. The burn deep in her core pulsed strongly, and she ground herself against the hard thick length of Andrés's arousal, her body instinctively seeking the hedonistic sensations of relief only he could provide, and it was without any conscious thought whatsoever that she lifted herself enough to sink down on his length.

'God… Gabrielle…' The last conscious part of Andrés tried to cut through…*holy Dios*…the pleasure of being completely bare inside her… and he'd thought the pleasure he'd found with her already had been the pinnacle… When her glazed eyes met his and thick spasms gripped him as her beautiful mouth parted to release the cries of her climax, he only just held on to that last wisp of consciousness to lift her off him.

He caught the confusion on her face before her eyes glittered, and, still straddling his lap, she wrapped her fingers around his arousal and brought him to his own climax.

Gabrielle's eyes flickered open to early sunlight. Andrés's arm was hooked around her belly, a leg draped over her thigh, his breathing deep and rhythmic.

There was a dull ache pounding in her head.

It had nothing on the heavy pounding in her chest.

She looked at her watch. Seven thirty a.m.

Tears prickled her eyes.

The night was over. It was time to go.

Carefully moving his arm off her, she slid away from his leg and sat up. The throbbing in her head even more acute, she looked around the vast room for something to cover herself.

A black towelling robe hung on the back of a door. She padded gingerly to it and slipped it on.

It smelled of Andrés. Its size drowned her.

Her chest filling, she crept out of the bedroom and into the bathroom opposite.

Her dress was neatly folded on a chair she barely remembered seeing before, shoes and clutch bag beside it. Andrés's discarded clothes, the champagne bottle and flutes had all vanished. The bathroom was as sparkling as it had been when she'd first set foot in it.

It was as if what they'd shared in there had never happened.

But it *had* happened, she thought, a sad smile pulling on her lips to remember just how amazing it had been.

She pulled the heavy velvet up to her waist, blinking more tears away.

Only when she'd put her arm through the sleeve and zipped the dress up did she allow herself to look in the full-length mirror. Her reflection shocked her. She'd expected to look different, that what she and Andrés had shared would have marked her in some obvious way, but it was still her face looking back at her.

She felt different. Changed.

Changed or not, she had her real life to return to where nothing had changed.

After several long breaths Gabrielle ran her fingers through her hair in an attempt to tidy it and noticed there was a gaping hole at the side of the dress where Andrés had ripped the clasp. A tear finally sprang free. She hastily wiped it away.

She supposed a touch of melancholy was to be expected after the night she'd just experienced.

Picking up her shoes and the clutch bag, she left the bathroom and padded back to Andrés's bedroom. Heart now thumping violently as the time to say goodbye drew near she pushed the door open.

Her heart sighed. He was still deep in sleep.

With another sigh, she took the whole room in properly for the first time, committing the dark blue fitted wardrobes and side boards, and velvet blue soft furnishings dominated by the huge bed to her memory.

It was a beautifully modern room she acknowledged with a deep pang, and that was the bed she'd given her virginity in, given it to a man she wished with all her heart…

She closed her eyes and forced her thoughts to where they should be, not to a place they should never go. Lucas was her priority. His safety and happiness were all that mattered.

Tiptoeing to Andrés, she carefully leaned over and placed a gentle kiss to his cheek.

His eyes sprang open.

He blinked a number of times before rolling onto his back. Patting the space next to him, his voice was thick with sleep. 'You're going?'

More choked than she'd imagined she'd be when she'd agreed to stay the night with him, she nodded, and perched her bottom on the bed.

He reached for her hand. 'I would drive you home…'

She threaded her fingers through his. 'You're probably over the limit.' Make that definitely.

His grin was rueful if pained. 'I think there's been an explosion in my head.'

She started to laugh but it hurt her own head too much. 'And mine.'

'It was worth it.' An intensity came into his stare. 'I had a great night, Gabrielle.'

She squeezed his fingers. 'Me too.'

It had been the best night of her life.

'Michael will give you a lift and arrange for your bike and things to be brought to you.'

'Thank you.' Leaning down, she kissed his mouth. 'Thank you for everything.'

Her intention to move away was scuppered when he caught the back of her head and kissed her so deeply and thoroughly that for a moment she didn't even feel her poorly head.

Grinning, he rested back on the pillow and hooked an arm above his head. Stretching his body quite clearly showed the delineation of his erection beneath the light grey silk bedsheet covering him to his waist.

'Sure you can't stay for a while longer?' he coaxed knowingly.

This time she did laugh, even as desire pulsed heavily inside her. Planting one last kiss to his mouth, she dragged herself back to her feet and shuffled to the door where she turned to face him one last time and blew him a kiss.

He pressed it to his lips and blew her a kiss back.

It was mid-morning when Andrés finally threw the covers off and dragged himself out of bed.

What a night.

Donning his robe, he laughed under his breath at just how fantastic the whole night had been. There was a very good chance he wouldn't kill his sister for manipulating him into it after all. An internal stop button when drinking meant he hadn't suffered many hangovers in his life but of the few he'd had, this was the only one that felt good. Even better, Gabrielle had left without any drama or hints about seeing him again. They'd both known exactly what the night was and that had been enough for them both. Still, he had to admit that if she hadn't needed to return home to her son, he'd have coaxed her into staying in bed with him. *Dios*, just to remember how fantastic the sex had been was enough to make him hard…

A mark on the light grey under-sheet suddenly caught his eye.

Pulling away the crumpled heap of silk sheets partially covering it, he looked a little more closely.

It was blood.

A shiny, futuristic car approached the border. Gabrielle's heart jumped. It was an automatic reaction that had occurred every time a car that vaguely looked the same as Andrés's arrived at the principality over the last five days. None of them had been his and nor was this one. The system that registered every non-domiciled person in the principality, and which she had access to as part of her job, showed he'd left Monte Cleure late on Sunday evening.

She wondered where he was. What he was doing…

An idle fantasy drifted into her vision of riding her bicycle in a floaty summer dress and a huge shiny car pulling to a stop beside her, and the window rolling down and…

'Gabrielle?'

Her colleague's voice pulled her out of her daydream.

'Sorry,' she muttered. 'I was miles away.'

Remi peered closely at her. 'Who is he?'

'What?'

'It's got to be a man. You've been smiling to yourself and falling away into your own little world all week.'

Mortified, aware she was blushing, Gabrielle shook her head. 'It's no one.'

Mercifully, three cars joined the manual passport check line and she was able to escape Remi's prying, but even as she made a concerted effort to get on with the job, her colleague's words rang continually in her ears.

Gabrielle had known all those years ago from the way Eloise kept smiling to herself that her sister had fallen for someone. It seemed that no time passed from those early dreamy smiles before she fell into the pure, deep love that would destroy her.

She wasn't Eloise, Gabrielle reminded herself.

Of course she'd fallen for Andrés, but it was a chemical thing, a lust thing involving the body and not the heart. One precious night of hedonism. It was over and now she needed to gently push him into the treasured memories part of her mind and stop his occupancy of it.

The Thursday morning traffic rush was over when Andrés left his Barcelona office complex and got straight into the waiting car. A short drive and he'd be in his helicopter and on his way to Monte Cleure. That was the plan until he stepped out of the car at his airfield and the hot mid-morning sun beamed down on him. The last few months had been so busy that he couldn't remember the last time he'd fed vitamin D straight into his flesh.

'You take the helicopter, I'm going to drive,' he impulsively told his entourage. He'd only driven the newest addition to his fleet of cars once and as it was currently being stored in the hangar here and he had the rest of the day free from meetings, why not take advantage of the freedom?

The shocked eyes of his PA, bodyguard and lawyer zipped to him before they all bustled into the helicopter. He could imagine what they'd be saying. Andrés hadn't driven himself on a working day in a decade. His trip to Monte Cleure was business. He had an early morning meeting with Nathaniel and the lawyers the next day to thrash out the final details of their latest joint business venture.

The roads to Monte Cleure were clearer than the last time he'd made this journey and, shades on and the music turned up loud, he put the roof down to enjoy the feel of warm air flying through his hair.

He thought back to the last time he'd made this journey, almost three weeks ago, and how his preoccupation with the paternity case had ruined what could have been a fun drive with his sister. Sophia had called him the evening after the party brimming with excitement and curiosity about how things had gone with Gabrielle. Andrés had taken great delight in not satisfying any of it other than to confirm that no, he hadn't made plans to see her again. His sister's disappointment at this had been palpable. She couldn't understand that the night with Gabrielle had been as perfect for its ending as it had been for the night itself. He had no wish to pursue a short-term fling with her and ruin that perfection with an inevitably bitter end and he'd sensed it was the same for Gabrielle. Their night together had been one of a kind, a memory to be treasured.

Traffic slowed to a crawl. He'd reached the queue for the border.

He wondered if Gabrielle was working. It was a thought that had floated in and out of his mind since getting in the car, although obviously had played no part at all in his impulsive decision to drive.

Smoothing his hair back, he cruised into the facial recognition line. As he inched forwards, he noted a car being searched but none of the staff undertaking it were Gabrielle.

Now at the front of the queue, he looked into the camera. A light went green, the barrier lifted and he crossed the border.

Gabrielle logged onto the system. Quickly checking that no one in the administration office was paying her any attention, she clicked the link that listed all the cars and every non-domiciled visitor currently in the principality. Having spent yesterday afternoon processing a drug-trafficker caught with methamphetamines in his wheel hubs, liaising with the police and then hurrying off to collect Lucas from nursery, this was her first opportunity to check since early yesterday morning. She had twenty-four hours' worth of data to scroll through and exactly ten minutes until her shift started to do it in.

It took two minutes until the name she'd been both praying and dreading to see appeared.

He was here. Finally. After four days of diligently checking the system whenever she could for his name, Andrés had passed the border at around the time she'd been in the processing unit carefully testing, weighing and recording the drug stash. Unless he'd since left the principality by helicopter, which the system was always a little slower to update, he was still here.

The nausea that had been rolling in her stomach for days on end rose up her throat. She covered her mouth and closed her eyes, willing it to pass.

'Is everything okay, Gabrielle?'

She opened her eyes to the concerned gaze of the shift manager. 'I'm sorry, I know this is terrible timing but I need to go.'

Her manager's stare became meditative as she waited for an explanation.

'Please?' Gabrielle whispered. She wouldn't lie and say she was ill—the sickness in her stomach was wholly fear. 'It's a personal matter. I wouldn't do this if it wasn't important.'

Eventually there was a nod. 'I'll get cover for you.'

She exhaled her relief. 'Thank you.'

'Is there anything I can do to help?'

Fighting tears, she sucked in a breath and shook her head.

No one could help her with what she needed to do.

CHAPTER NINE

THE CONTRACTS OF his new business venture with Nathaniel signed, his stomach filled with the exquisite food served by the palace's talented chefs over a late lunch, Andrés peered out of the car window at Monte Cleure's bustling pristine streets, tuned out the talk between the staff travelling with him, and contemplated the rest of the day that lay ahead of him. Two video conferences, one for the forthcoming Janson Media AGM and one with the acquisition team in Japan for his buyout of a cutting-edge Manga publishing company that had, in the last twenty-four hours, hit unexpected roadblocks. Hopefully it would all be sorted before he left for the evening get-together at the private members' club. By rights, he should take a date with him, should already have organised one. It was a task he'd kept putting off and now it was too late to get anything organised. That was okay. He didn't mind that all the others in the group he was meeting with would be paired up, and the great thing about Club Giroud was that it was no gentleman's club—rich, successful women were equally drawn to it. Andrés had met three previous lovers in Club Giroud's various incarnations across Europe. It was about time he found himself another lover. Tonight would be an excellent place to start.

His mind drifted to Gabrielle. It had drifted to her numerous times since their night together. Numerous times he'd been tempted to get in contact and offer to fly her out to him because, *Dios*, his veins still thrummed from their lovemaking. Nights were the worst. He couldn't seem to stop his mind from reliving the pleasure they'd shared which only ramped up the thrumming in his veins that no amount of self-care seemed able to alleviate.

But just as he'd resisted reaching out to fly her to him, so too would he resist calling to see what her plans for the evening were…

A small figure hunched on the doorstep of the rear entry into his apartment building pulled him sharply from his thoughts. Craning his head back, the position of the car as it turned into the underground car park made it impossible to see for certain but that didn't stop his hand hitting the intercom and Andrés commanding his driver to stop.

Gabrielle had watched so many chauffeur-driven cars come and go from the Imperium's underground car park that she'd lost count. Once they were swallowed inside it, the guarded doors closed and she had no chance of following. All she could do was sit there and hope Andrés went in or out before she had to collect Lucas, and pray that he noticed her. If he didn't or time ran away from her then she'd leave a message with the concierge for him to call her. She hoped it didn't come to that. What she had to tell him needed to be done in person.

Time almost had run away from her when the enormous Range Rover came to an abrupt halt at the halfway point of its turn into the car park. Her heart and legs kicked into gear before her brain did, pumping wildly as she hurried to it, and so it was that when he emerged from the back, everything she'd spent the past days going over in her head dissolved.

The reality of Andrés in the flesh after nearly three weeks of memory came as a powerful shock.

Dressed in a clearly bespoke dark grey suit, everything about him was so much more than she'd remembered, from his height and breadth—he towered over her—to the dark olive hue of his skin and the blackness of his hair, even the depth of his voice when he warmly said, 'This is a pleasant surprise. Are you here to see me?'

Her senses overwhelmed with the man who'd haunted her waking and sleeping dreams since she'd left his bed, Gabrielle nodded.

'You should have waited in the atrium. It's far more comfortable.'

She had to swallow to loosen her vocal cords. 'I was afraid I'd miss you.' The concierge—not Bernard this time—and the other staff member had taken one look at her work uniform and wrinkled their noses in unison. They'd been spectacularly unhelpful. One had called the apartment and spoken to Michael to establish that Andrés wasn't in but refused to assist in any other way, including a refusal to let Gabrielle speak to Michael herself and at least know if Andrés was planning to return to his apartment that day.

The fizzing bolt that had shot through Andrés to realise that it really was Gabrielle on the step slipped away as he took in the pallor of her skin and the nervous, almost frightened energy she vibrated with.

Folding his arms slowly across his chest, he looked at her more closely. 'What's wrong?'

'Can we go somewhere private, please? I need to talk to you about something.'

His concern growing, he indicated the open door of his car. 'Get in.'

He followed her into it. The last time they'd shared the back of a car together, it had been only the two of them. This time his PA, lawyer and PA's assistant were with them, all pretending it was perfectly normal for a frazzled young woman in a border guard uniform and clumpy boots to join them, a pretence they kept up when the car was parked moments later in Andrés's designated bay and maintained in the elevator ride to his penthouse. Inside, they disappeared to his offices to get back onto the phone with the team in Japan while he led Gabrielle into the main living room, the beats of his heart now painful weighty thumps.

In all his imaginings—and of course he'd had idle fantasies about running into Gabrielle again, passing her in the street, spotting her from the window of a restaurant, sometimes riding her bicycle, always with her hair loose, an irreverent laugh that only she knew the meaning behind a whisper away from escaping her pillowy lips. He'd imagined her double take when she spotted him, the smile that would spread across her face, the knowing look that would pass between them…

He'd never imagined those pillowy lips could be pulled so thin or that hair scraped back in a neat ponytail could conversely be messy and unkempt. She was holding herself so rigidly a jolt would snap her in half. Something was clearly wrong and he hoped like hell it wasn't anything to do with her son. In the few idle hours he'd had since his last visit to Monte Cleure he'd researched the principality's social system and learned that citizens were entitled to only the most basic health care.

Finally alone, he was about to ask again what the matter was when her dark eyes suddenly locked onto his. 'I'm pregnant.'

Her words landed like a cold punch in his guts that spread like ice straight into his brain.

Gabrielle watched the colour drain from Andrés's face. She watched the emotions flicker over his handsome features in slow motion, incomprehension slowly morphing into stunned disbelief and then back into incomprehension.

'That isn't possible,' he dragged out hoarsely.

She forced herself to maintain eye contact. 'I took two tests on Monday.'

She'd known even before she was a day late that something was happening to her. She'd buried her head in the sand for two days, telling herself that swollen, tingly breasts this close to her period was nothing to worry about, then spent three further days hitting the toilet at increasingly frequent intervals, desperately waiting for blood to appear.

His colour was slowly returning, the incomprehension of his stare slowly dissipating as his clever brain began to turn and his eyes narrowed.

'It's yours,' she confirmed before he could

voice the cynical thoughts she could see rotating in his mind.

A moment passed between them, a flash where she could see into his thoughts and knew he was remembering the bath they'd shared, when she'd lost all control of herself and sank onto him without protection.

Her cheeks flamed and pelvis contracted, just as they did every time she made herself remember that moment. Had it happened then, even though he'd lifted her off him? That was the question she'd tortured herself with. The hour or so before they'd finally passed out wrapped in each other's arms was still a potted blur of hedonistic champagne-fuelled memories.

How could she have been so reckless and irresponsible?

And how could she be standing only feet away from him with her heart thrashing so wildly and an increasingly desperate yearn to throw herself into his arms and beg him to tell her everything would be okay?

Feelings like this were dangerous.

Once Andrés accepted he was the father he'd want to be involved. He'd said as much at the party, that the reason he didn't want children was because he'd want to be there every day for them, therefore binding him and the child's

mother for life. It was being bound to a woman
for life he found so repellent and the reason his
acceptance of paternity would only come with
cast iron proof. Gabrielle accepted this and had
prepared herself for it. What she hadn't anticipated was all the emotions swelling in her at
being with him again.

Only by bringing Lucas to the forefront of
her mind, just as she'd done every time she'd
felt the panic starting to rise and consume her,
was she able to clamp down on the swell and
dredge the words she'd rehearsed for this moment. Her little boy had suffered too much in
his short life already without the only mother
he'd ever known falling apart. Gabrielle remembered all too clearly how her mother had fallen
apart when her father died and could never put
Lucas through anything like that.

'I know this is a shock for you and that you're
not going to take my word that the baby's yours,'
she said as calmly as she could manage. 'I accept that you will want to wait until it's born
and a DNA test can be done before acknowl-
edging paternity, but this baby *is* yours. I don't
have a lawyer but I will comply with any test
your legal team asks of me so long as it isn't
harmful to the baby.'

She had to swallow bile to force the last words

out. 'I also want to make it clear that there is no way I'm going to have an abortion.'

The mannequin called Andrés who'd listened to her pre-prepared speech without moving so much as a facial muscle came to life. The narrowed eyes glittered, the handsome face darkening as he moved towards her.

Gripping her arms in an effort to control her trembles, Gabrielle tried not to feel guilty for her assumption that he would want her to take the easy way out. The one thing she knew about rich men was their belief that cash made all problems go away. Lucas's father had offered cash for a termination and while the only thing Andrés had in common with The Bastard was his wealth—even his arrogance was of a different hue—she would not take the risk. Better she be upfront and say an abortion was not on the cards than experience the pain of him suggesting it, even if it was an eminently sensible suggestion. Sensible or not, Gabrielle could never do that, a notion that had crystalised when she'd walked Lucas to the beach an hour after the tests had both proved positive and she'd looked at his little hand clutched so trustingly in hers and imagined the little hands forming inside her.

Little hands created by the most passionate and wonderful night of her life, and as she gazed into Andrés's glittering eyes, she had to hold herself even more tightly as the fear of his denouncing of her and the life they'd created together grew even stronger.

Whatever Andrés had intended to say to her was forgotten by a loud rap on the door behind her. The woman who'd been in the car with him burst into the room waving a phone, closely followed by the other two from the car, one of whom she now recognised as the lawyer who'd drafted the non-disclosure agreement.

'Sorry to interrupt,' the woman said, thrusting the phone into Andrés's hand, 'but Kaito will be calling in one minute. You need to talk to him—he's learned that members of the board are trying to kill the deal.'

The curse that flew from Andrés's mouth made the woman's eyes widen in shock. Even the men looked taken aback.

Only Gabrielle knew the curse wasn't aimed at the deal being killed but at herself and the situation she'd just hit him with.

The phone rang in his hand.

Nostrils flaring, jaw tight, he looked at it before his eyes pinned back on Gabrielle.

'Take the call,' she said, almost weak with relief at the timely interruption.

He held her stare for a few more loaded moments before jerking a nod and putting the phone to his ear. 'Kaito? What the hell is going on?'

With one more hard stare at Gabrielle, he disappeared from the living room flanked by his minions.

Dragging his legs to the bar, Andrés poured himself three fingers of bourbon and downed it. Then he poured himself another hefty measure, drank half, and had another read of the note Gabrielle had left for him.

Dear Andrés,

Sorry for leaving but I need to collect Lucas from nursery. My mother's taking him to France tomorrow for a few days if you want to talk things through? Will understand if you'd rather go through your legal team.

Gabrielle

Head spinning, he went over her spiel again. Remembered the way she'd held herself. Her fear. Her bravery… The way she'd spoken to him as if they hadn't shared the most unbelievably perfect night together.

All her assumptions.

He took another large drink and sloshed it around his teeth, thinking hard through his

spinning head for the reason his initial gut reaction had been that it was impossible for Gabrielle to be pregnant.

A tap on the door that connected the living
room with the offices brought him back in the
room.

His PA peered in. 'The team in Japan agree
with Kaito—you're needed in Tokyo or the deal
will be lost. Lara's arranging the flight slots
now—we should get you in the air within the
hour.'

She disappeared without expecting a response. She didn't expect a response because
it was unthinkable that Andrés would do anything but fly to Japan to salvage a deal he'd long
coveted and which he'd already spent millions
in legal fees and other sundries on.

He threw the rest of the bourbon down his
throat and headed to his offices.

An air of efficiency pervaded the room, lap-
tops and tablets being packed into briefcases,
translation apps being updated. His closest staff
were well used to crossing continents without
any notice. It was why he paid them such hefty
salaries. That and their uncanny business acu-
men.

'I'm not going.'

They all looked at him with a variant of the

look they'd given when he'd announced he'd drive himself into Monte Cleure.

'I'm taking the weekend off.'

His PA was the first to speak. 'But... Kaito said...'

'I don't care. The three of you go and do the best you can to save the deal. I've got something much more important to deal with.'

Gabrielle put her mug of hot chocolate on the small pine coffee table, turned the television on with the remote and, exhausted, sank onto the sofa.

She flicked through the channels looking for something to catch her eye but all the titles were a blur.

She knew the sensible thing would be to go to bed even though it was much earlier than her usual bedtime but the thought of lying down and being alone with her thoughts...

All her thoughts made her want to cry.

Selecting the comforting familiarity of an action film she'd watched so many times she could recite the words, Gabrielle cuddled a cushion to her belly, snuggled down and tried to lose herself in it.

She'd thought telling Andrés would be a relief after the dread she'd carried all these days, but if anything she felt worse. Being with Andrés in the flesh, in all his physicality… She could still feel the longing that had gripped her, the ache deep in her bones…

She hadn't expected it to be that strong. That intense.

Maybe it was for the best that things would be handled through his lawyers until paternity was confirmed to his satisfaction. It would give her the time she needed to really get a handle on the emotions thrashing through her. She'd left the ball in his court about talking things through but held little hope that—

There was a knock on her door.

Startled, she lifted her head and looked at her watch. Eight p.m. She rarely had unannounced visitors during the day never mind in the evening.

The second knock shifted her off the sofa.

She put her eye to the spyhole. Her heart thumped so hard she reared back.

It was Andrés.

Andrés had lifted his fist to rap on the door for a third time when he heard the distinctive click of a door being unlocked.

Gabrielle's shocked face appeared.

His chest tightening, he took her in, the faded jeans, the loose white top that had slipped off a shoulder reminding him of the dress she'd dazzled him in at the party, the thick dark hair worn loose but no neater than it had been earlier, the bare feet with the pretty painted toenails.

Dark brown eyes wide with apprehension, her voice was shaky as she whispered, 'What are you doing here?'

'You have to ask?' he said tersely. 'Are you going to let me in?'

Top teeth slicing into her bottom lip, she looked over her shoulder and then back at him with a pained shake of her head. 'Lucas is in bed. Let's talk tomorrow after my mum's collected him or we can—'

'We talk now.' Gabrielle had delivered her bombshell news four hours ago. In the intervening hours he'd likely destroyed the Japanese buyout, a setback to his Asia expansion plans that should not be underestimated, and likely destroyed the flooring of his apartment with all his pacing as he'd put his runaway thoughts into order. The thought of waiting one more minute was intolerable.

'He's a really light sleeper, and this isn't something he should overhear.'

Andrés leaned forwards and pitched his voice as low as it would go, enunciating every word so there could be no misunderstanding. 'If you don't let me in right now, I will file a report with the authorities that you are passing someone else's child off as your own.'

CHAPTER TEN

BLACK SPOTS FILLED Gabrielle's vision.

Hot, rabid blood filled her head.

A deep voice that brooked no argument echoed in her ears. 'Last chance, Gabrielle. Let me in.'

The world was swimming around her.

Only the image of her son, tucked up in his bed, enabled her feet to move.

Andrés knew from Gabrielle's ashen face that he'd put the pieces of the jigsaw together correctly, all the thoughts that had raced through his mind as he'd paced his apartment, impressions of their night together coalescing and solidifying into the only possible explanation.

He stepped into a narrow entrance hall with a bicycle hung on the wall and closed the door behind him. One glance in the open-plan living space was all it took to take in the small kitchen area and the small dining table that separated it from the living area, which consisted of a small sofa, an armchair, a television, a high book case crammed with well-thumbed paperbacks, and a large box crammed with toys. The whole living area could fit in his main Monte Cleure bathroom. Like the building the apartment was homed in, everything was old but clean and well looked after, little touches lifting it into something cosy and inviting. It reminded him of his childhood apartment.

All this he processed without conscious thought, his attention fully taken with the woman pregnant with his child, who was now standing against a freestanding fridge looking like she was about to collapse.

'Why don't you sit down?' he suggested curtly.

'Who's that man, Mummy?'

A small, tousle-haired child in too-short superhero pyjamas had appeared from the corridor to the side of the living area.

It was the waking version of the sleeping child he'd seen on the screen of Gabrielle's phone at the party.

The boy's appearance brought Gabrielle to life. She dove to him quicker than a sprinter at the sound of a starting gun and scooped him into her arms.

'You should be asleep,' she scolded, holding him tightly and smothering his cheek with kisses.

He wriggled and looked over her shoulder at Andrés. 'A noise woke me. Who is he, Mummy?'

'I'm Andrés,' he said in French with a wave, doing his best to appear non-threatening to the child who was clearly unsettled at the strange man in his apartment. He had to think of the correct French to add, 'I'm a friend of your mother's.'

Dark brown eyes narrowed with suspicion at Andrés before he put a palm to Gabrielle's cheek. 'Why is he here?'

'To see me,' she answered, shifting his weight to her hip.

'Why?'

'Because he's a friend, and friends sometimes like to visit each other. Your friends from nursery come to play with you, don't they?'

He considered this. 'Are you going to play a game with him?'

'No. He'll be leaving in a few minutes. Come on, let's get you back to bed.'

As she started walking, the boy put his face on Gabrielle's shoulder then lifted it again to look at Andrés. 'Goodnight,' he said before his thumb disappeared into his mouth.

Andrés would have thought he was too choked to smile but he managed to raise one for this little boy. 'Goodnight, Lucas. It was nice to meet you.'

Gabrielle tucked Lucas under his duvet and kissed his forehead. 'Goodnight, my sweet.'

His big trusting eyes held hers. 'Mummy, is that man my daddy?'

How she held back the tears at this question she would never know. Lucas had only asked about his father once, shortly after he'd started nursery. She'd truthfully told him that his daddy lived in another country, and had been filled with gratitude that he'd asked no more. More questions would come one day. Until a few minutes ago she'd thought the worst thing would be still not knowing how to answer them. Now terror had struck her heart that she might not be the one to answer them at all, and she had to concentrate with everything not to let the fresh swimming in her head sink her.

'No,' she whispered.

How did Andrés know? How was it possible that he'd discovered the truth?

It *wasn't* possible.

Lucas's skinny arms hooked around her neck. 'Can I have another story?'

She kissed his nose and swallowed back tears. 'It's late and you need to get some sleep. I'll read you one in the morning.'

He smacked a kiss to her lips.

After a dozen more kisses and a dozen '*I love you*'s, Gabrielle left her son on the cusp of sleep and gently closed his door.

Hand pressed to her racing heart, the sickness churning in her stomach making the nausea from telling Andrés about the pregnancy seem like a tepid test run, she lifted her chin and straightened her spine.

As terrified as she'd ever been in her life but filled with all the fight that had enabled her to get through these last four years, she found Andrés examining the photos displayed on the walls of the living section.

Andrés turned his head to her. 'I'm sorry for waking him.'

Lucas's appearance had dampened much of the angst and fury that had propelled him to Gabrielle's apartment.

Guilt lay heavily in him, a guilt that had been steadily growing while he waited for Gabrielle to put the boy to bed and his attention had become increasingly captured by her photographs. The walls were crammed with them, ranging from her childhood to the present day, plenty of full family pictures from when her father, a smiling man Gabrielle bore a strong resemblance to, had been alive, going as far back as her parents' wedding day. All the most recent ones featured Lucas, starting from when he could have only been days old. Most were of him with Gabrielle, but there were some too of him with the woman he already recognised as

Gabrielle's mother and a couple of others with the man he recognised as her brother.

He kept going back to one particular picture of the three Breton children sitting in descending age order like a caterpillar, Gabrielle barely a toddler, and comparing it to one of the most recent Lucas pictures. The resemblance between Lucas and the other Bretons was obvious but with Gabrielle's brother, the resemblance was unmistakable. Lucas could be his doppelgänger.

The longer he'd looked at the pictures, the harder the pulse in his temple had throbbed. A hazy memory kept playing in his mind of the cloud of sadness that had enveloped Gabrielle during that brief mention of her sister when they'd been sharing a bath. She'd blinked the sadness away and replaced it with a seduction so hedonistic he'd been closer than he'd ever been in his life to saying to hell with the need for protection.

The irony of her being pregnant despite his self-denial was strong.

It had been the seductive hedonism he'd lived over in his mind since, forgetting that brief cloud, and now that cloud was all he could see.

There was a steely determination in the dark eyes locked on him which carried into her walk as she strode to stand before him. She pitched her voice low but strength resonated in it. 'Andrés, you need to leave. We can't talk with Lucas around, you must see that.'

He thought of the way the little boy had palmed Gabrielle's cheek, and the pulse in his temple beat harder than ever. As much as he wanted to shake answers out of the woman pregnant with his child, that little boy sleeping his innocent sleep had burrowed into his conscience.

Breathing heavily, he rubbed the back of his neck. 'What time is your mother collecting him tomorrow?'

'At eight.'

'I'll be here for nine.'

She closed her eyes. 'Thank you.'

Keeping a few paces behind him, she walked him to the door.

Once he'd crossed the threshold, she called his name.

He turned back to her.

The steel in her eyes blazed stronger than ever. 'I don't know what you think you know, but Lucas *is* my son, and there is nothing I wouldn't do to protect him, so don't you ever threaten me with him again.'

A lump lodged in his throat. He thought again of the small boy in the too-small superhero pyjamas palming Gabrielle's cheek. The love and trust in that gesture.

He thought too, of the undeniable familial similarity between them. The photos crammed all over her walls.

And then he looked more closely into the steely eyes and for the flash of a moment was transported back in time. It wasn't steel ringing at him but fire. The fierceness of Gabrielle's love for her son was the same fierce love for their children that had kept his parents together when it would have been better for them to go their separate ways.

He understood in that flash of a moment that Gabrielle really would do anything to protect Lucas and that that same fierce love would be used to protect the child developing inside her.

His child. Their child.

His heart twisted.

'Gabrielle, I give you my word that I will never make such a threat again. Lucas is your son, I can see that.' Holding her stare, he dropped his voice to a murmur. 'But you and I both know you didn't give birth to him.'

Gabrielle climbed into the back of the car feeling as wretched and sick as she'd ever felt, a sensation not helped by the scent of Andrés's cologne diving straight into her bloodstream and making her pulse surge before her bottom had even made contact with the leather seat.

It shouldn't be like this, she thought miserably. Not only was Andrés far richer and far more powerful than The Bastard, but somehow he knew the truth about Lucas. He had the power to destroy her entire world. It shouldn't be possible that she could still feel so drawn to him and that she should be so acutely aware of the muscular tanned arms and the sleeve tattoo on display in the khaki polo shirt he was wearing. It was disconcerting to find him wearing smart tan shorts too. She'd assumed he only owned suits and tuxedos. Or was this all just her fevered mind going into overdrive after a night of tossing and turning?

He nodded a greeting to her. 'Did Lucas and your mother get away okay?'

She could hardly work her throat to answer. 'Yes.'

This was the second year in a row her mother had taken Lucas to France and waving goodbye had been just as bittersweet for Gabrielle as it had been last year. Bitter because being in the apartment without him felt like she'd had a limb removed. Sweet because the bond between grandma and grandson was so strong. They might not have much in the way of riches but one thing Lucas had been raised with was an abundance of love.

She cleared her throat. 'Where are we going?'

Andrés's driver had headed off in the wrong direction to his apartment.

'Somewhere neutral.'

'Why neutral?'

'Because I suspect the conversation we're going to have will be difficult for us both.'

Her stomach dropped.

Breathing deeply, she gazed out of the window and ordered herself not to panic.

She could laugh. She'd told herself not to panic at least every ten seconds since Andrés had left her apartment. It frightened her how much she wanted to trust the sincerity she'd seen in his eyes when he'd sworn never to use Lucas as a threat again, but even if she could trust it, there was nothing to stop him carrying out his threat to report her to the authorities. She had everything she needed to back up her lies to them—and she would lie to the Queen of Monte Cleure herself if the alternative meant losing Lucas—but if they ordered a DNA test all the lies and documents supporting them would come to nothing.

How did Andrés know? That was another thing she couldn't get over. The secret had been kept tight for four years.

'We are here,' he said, breaking through her rabid thoughts.

Somewhere neutral turned out to be the harbour.

They walked in silence down the jetty to a gleaming yacht, one of the biggest docked there.

'Is this yours?' she asked, unable to imagine Andrés bothering to invest his money on a superyacht she doubted his workaholic lifestyle gave him the time to enjoy.

'Yes.'

'Then how can it be neutral?'

'Because I've not spent any time on it since the day I took delivery of it.'

'Seriously?'

He raised a broad shoulder. 'Sophia went on and on at me until I gave in and bought it. You can blame her for the interior decoration. All my family enjoy using it. The rest of the time it's chartered out. It was pure luck that it was docked in Barcelona.'

Climbing the steps that had been lowered for them, the professional crew greeted them with glasses of freshly squeezed orange juice.

The interior decoration was tastefully extravagant and Gabrielle easily imagined the rich colours and plush furnishings coming from Sophia's creative imagination. If her stomach wasn't so tight and cramped with nerves of what was going to come, her mouth would be open in stunned appreciation at yet more evidence of how the super wealthy lived.

This yacht that had to have cost around the

hundred million mark, had essentially been bought as a gift for Andrés's family to enjoy.

By the time they'd settled on the sprawling sun deck with an array of breakfast food and fruit and drinks laid out for them, the captain had already set sail and the harbour was a speck in the distance behind them.

Nibbling on a chocolate brioche roll, Gabrielle tried to regulate her breathing, a feat not made easy with Andrés sitting across the table from her nursing a coffee. She hadn't thought to bring sunglasses with her and with his eyes hidden behind a pair of aviators that perfectly suited him, she felt strangely exposed. At least she'd changed from her faithful jeans into her only summer dress, a floaty, modest thigh length cream creation that dipped in a V to skim her cleavage and matched perfectly with her ballet shoes. It had been a last-minute panicking change made after Lucas and her mother had driven away that she couldn't explain any more than she could explain the application of mascara and lip gloss and the extra conditioner used to defrizz her hair.

Armour, she told herself. It was going to be hard enough getting through the day without feeling like a bag lady, especially when pitted against the dark masculine perfection that was Andrés.

How could someone grow more beautiful each time you set eyes on them?

'How did you know about Lucas?' she asked when she couldn't bear another second of the loaded silence. All her emotions had coiled so tightly that she could feel them trying to break free. She *had* to keep herself together.

Andrés put his coffee on the table and stretched his neck. It had been a long night, his overloaded brain making way for sleep in snatches, memories of their night together colliding with thoughts of the future he'd never wanted.

His life as he knew it was over.

Gabrielle was carrying his child.

He'd be tied to her for ever.

Amidst all the turmoil of his thoughts was the indisputable fact that she was passing off someone else's child as her own, and until he knew for certain that Lucas hadn't been snatched from his real mother, coming up with a game plan for their own child was out of the question.

The visit to Gabrielle's apartment had given him a good idea of who the child really belonged to but he needed it confirmed, needed to hear all the reasons why.

One look at her ashen face when she'd climbed into his car and the grim determination to drag all the answers from her that he'd set off with had melted away.

To see the wry, determined, intelligent, fun woman he'd spent the best night of his life with in such clear turmoil and distress did something to him. It was similar to how he used to feel when growing up at Sophia's distress, as if her distress was his distress. To have similar feelings…similar but far more acute…for Gabrielle had been disconcerting in the extreme. It had knocked him off his stride.

Up here on the sun deck, with the rising sun landing like jewels on Gabrielle's skin just as the setting sun had done the night of the party, his tastebuds tingled to remember the sweetness of that skin, his fingers tingled to remember its smooth, soft texture, his loins tingled to remember the sweet, hedonistic perfection of their night together, and the questions had melted even further away.

And now her quietly delivered question had pulled him back to the here and now.

'It was an educated guess but your reaction confirmed it,' he said tightly.

A line appeared in her forehead and she shook her head. 'But… How could you guess something like that?'

'There was a smear of blood on my sheets.'

Her eyes widened, colour saturating her face.

'I assumed at the time that it was menstrual blood and that you must have started your period.' As his hangover had worn off and the haziness of the night cleared, Andrés had been glad of that stain. They'd used protection but they'd been careless. Gabrielle starting her period had put any worries about their carelessness to bed.

He'd never been in the slightest bit careless before that night. Not ever.

That she'd conceived that night meant the chances of it being menstrual blood was reduced to practically zero, and as soon as that fact lodged in his brain, it brought fresh insight to everything else, including the lack of physical evidence that she'd carried or given birth to a child. That there was not a single photo of Gabrielle pregnant on her walls had only added weight to this.

'You were a virgin.'

Dark eyes swimming with unshed tears, pretty chin wobbling, her nod was barely perceptible.

His chest sharpened to remember the gasp she'd made when he'd entered her for the first time. That gasp hadn't been the shock of pleasure like he'd experienced but the shock of pain. If he'd known he'd have been gentle with her, so, so gentle.

'Is he your sister's?'

Her lips clamped together but the widening of her eyes let him know he'd hit the mark.

'He's obviously a Breton,' he said. 'There are many photos of Eloise displayed on your walls but none with him.' No photos of Eloise at all after Lucas's birth...

Blinking frantically, she got unsteadily to her feet and staggered to the railing, holding it tightly as she stared out over the endless sea.

Andrés stood beside her, waiting for her to speak, the sharpening of his chest a physical pain to witness the great gulps of air she was taking in.

He hated that this was so necessary.

Eventually, she said, 'Lucas *is* mine. I'm named as his mother on his birth certificate. He's been mine since he took his first breath.'

'Tell me what happened.'

Her voice caught. 'I can't.'

'I can't help if you don't tell me.'

'I don't need help.'

'Gabrielle, you only agreed to accompany me as my date that night because it was the perfect storm of timing for you.' Andrés spoke slowly, his words forming as they formulated in his mind. 'Lucas was with your mother and you'd been offered an invitation to the party of the century with a man you believed to be happily married, all arranged with his wife's urging. If you'd had the slightest idea of what would happen between us, you would have refused to be my date and no amount of bribery or coaxing would have caused you to change your mind. Am I wrong?'

Eyes now locked on his, she shook her head.

'If Lucas is legally yours then how is it that something—or someone—has frightened you into hiding away?'

'Not hiding,' she refuted. 'I have a job. Lucas goes to nursery and will be starting school in a few months. We do all the normal things that normal people do.'

'You were a twenty-three-year-old virgin,' he pointed out bluntly. 'That is not normal, not for a woman as sensual as you. Your life revolves entirely around Lucas. Everything you do is for him.'

'It's called being a mother.'

'It's called hiding from intimacy.'

Gabrielle looked back out over the calming sea and filled her lungs with the salty air. What was the point in fighting it any more?

Andrés already knew the bare bones of the truth. To entrust the rest of it to him…

She'd entrusted her virginity to him. She'd given the whole of herself to him that night and he'd given the whole of himself to her.

She'd told him about their baby expecting

him to denounce her and refuse to accept paternity until he had cast iron proof but he believed her. He'd questioned *how* she could be pregnant but he hadn't questioned his paternity. He'd accepted her at her word.

He could have taken his suspicions about Lucas straight to the authorities. His power meant they would have taken his suspicions seriously. The truth and his power could easily find Gabrielle in the situation of losing both her children. He could gain sole custody of their child and never have to bother with the thing he wanted the least—being tied to a woman for the rest of his life.

Just as on some basic level he must trust her, so too, she realised, did she trust him because as all the thoughts of what he could do swirled in her mind, a certainty grew in her that he would never do them.

She took possibly the deepest breath of her life and said, 'Lucas's father is a nasty, evil, rich bastard, and if his name is ever made public, he will have him taken from me.'

CHAPTER ELEVEN

GABRIELLE EXHALED. She'd said it. She'd rubbed the lamp and let the Genie out. And as she made that exhale, she heard Andrés take a sharp intake of breath.

Fixing her gaze on the horizon, she said, 'You need to understand what Eloise was like to understand it all. You see, she was always different. Her brain never worked the same as other people's. Monte Cleure has terrible mental health provisions—it was worse when we were ruled by King Dominic and his father before him, but I honestly think all the provisions in the world wouldn't have helped. Her brain was just wired differently, like there was something missing in it, if that makes sense? She was the sweetest, most loving person you could meet but she just couldn't process her emotions— the slightest thing would upset her and send her into a spiral of screams and tears and self-harm. When our father died she had to be hospitalised until she wasn't a danger to herself any more.' She closed her eyes, remembering how her mother too had fallen apart at the seams at the agony of losing her soul mate.

'She was so beautiful,' she continued quietly. 'Men always looked twice at her but The Bastard was the first man *she* ever noticed, and she was so excited for her first date. I imagined a sweet teenager but instead this man in his thirties wearing typical rich man yachting clothes turned up. It was obvious to me that he thought he was living dangerously by inviting a girl from Monte Cleure's poor district on a date. Most people sensed Eloise's vulnerabilities but I didn't trust that he'd picked up on them so I made sure he knew she had certain issues and that he needed to treat her kindly. He treated her so kindly that when she fell pregnant, he dumped her on the spot and wanted nothing to do with her or the baby. He told her she was unfit to be a mother and demanded she abort it.'

She felt Andrés stiffen.

'I had to threaten him with the press to make him take responsibility, but he gave her a wedge of hush money and tricked her into signing a contract forbidding her from ever making contact with him again or naming him as the father with the penalty for breaking it being that he'd take custody of the baby he didn't even want and force her to repay the money.'

At this, Andrés hissed a particularly crude curse under his breath.

'Yes, he is,' Gabrielle agreed. 'That bastard's treatment of her and his rejection of their child broke her, and she spiralled. She stopped eating, never left the apartment, her health deteriorated… I deferred university to care for her because we didn't dare leave her alone, and then on one of her lucid days, she sat down with me and Maman and told us she loved her baby too much to put it at risk of being a mother to it and that she wanted me to have it. She wouldn't listen to reason or take no for an answer, and worked herself up into such a state…' She squeezed her eyes shut to drive out the image of her beautiful sister screaming and hitting herself. 'What else could I do but agree?'

'Couldn't your mother have…?'

'Eloise wanted it to be me. She was adamant. She knew I wouldn't be allowed to adopt the baby because of my age—you have to be twenty-five to adopt in Monte Cleure, even if it's a family member and even with the consent of the mother—so it had to be made out that the baby was mine. She was insistent.'

'But why not your mother?'

'Because I was her protector and she trusted me more than anyone. Our mother took our father's death very badly and when Eloise fell apart over it too, it was me and Romeo who got her the help she needed because our mother couldn't even get out of bed.'

Andrés felt sick. Hadn't Gabrielle said her father died when she was ten? What a burden for a child of that age to endure. When he'd been that age and terrified of his parents' divorcing, he'd never had to fear losing one of them let alone both of them.

'So you agreed to pass the baby as yours.'

'I had to. No one outside the immediate family knew Eloise was pregnant. We told a few reliable gossips that I'd got pregnant after a fling with a tourist and they reliably spread the word. I started stuffing cushions under my clothes to mimic pregnancy... Honestly, I look back and wonder how I could have done it but it felt vitally necessary at the time, and my agreement calmed her. She stopped self-harming and started eating. Started showering again. When she was eight months gone, we did a moonlight flit to France so none of the neighbours saw that the wrong sister was pregnant, and rented a house close to a maternity hospital. When Eloise gave her details, she gave my name. We looked enough alike that my passport was accepted as identification.'

With fresh tears welling, Gabrielle took a moment to compose herself, only to jolt as warm fingers pressed lightly on her hand, an unspoken gesture of comfort that made her aching heart swell and gave her the strength to continue.

Turning her hand so their fingers threaded together, she took a deep breath and said, 'The birth went reasonably well. There were complications but she coped better than I could have hoped, and, Andrés, I swear to you she was happy, really happy, and completely smitten with him. She chose Lucas's name, changed his first nappy and when we returned to the house two days later to continue her recovery, she gave him to me. By then I was comfortable with the idea of being named as his mother but I fully expected we would all go home together and raise the baby between the three of us.'

'What happened?' The gentle squeeze of his fingers told her he'd already guessed what came next.

'She developed an infection.' Unthinkingly, Gabrielle rested her head against his arm, and dropped her voice. 'She didn't tell us that she was feeling unwell, just said that she was tired. She hid it so well and by the time we realised there was something wrong it was too late. We called for an ambulance and she was admitted to hospital but there was nothing they could do for her.'

The fingers threaded through hers tightened but he didn't speak.

'She slipped away from us.' A tear fell down her cheek. 'And the thing I remember most clearly is how peaceful she looked. Eloise suppressed her worst instincts for months to get Lucas safely into this world and then she let go.'

And with that, Gabrielle let go too, the tears she'd hardly been aware of holding back unleashing in a flood as the coil holding all her emotions tightly in place snapped.

Wiping her face frantically was futile, the blinding waterfall pouring down her cheeks an impossible force, but still she tried to stem the flow, right until strong arms wrapped around her and she found herself crying into Andrés's rock hard chest.

Oh, that wonderful familiar scent...

It only made her cry harder.

How could it be so familiar when all they'd spent was one night together? How could it be so *comforting*?

He held her tightly, mouth pressed into the top of her head, hands stroking her back, whispering words of comfort that she couldn't hear through the sound of her own blubbing but which acted like salve to her wounded heart.

Andrés had dealt with many feminine tears throughout the years but this was the first time each sob had landed like a blow to his own heart.

The burden of release, he guessed. Gabrielle had been carrying her secret and the pain of her sister's death for a very long time.

It took a long time for the tears to run dry and for Gabrielle to rub her cheek into his sodden chest and sigh. Making no effort to let go of him, her voice stronger, she said, 'Lucas was six months old when we ran into his father on the promenade. He was outside dining with a woman and saw us out walking. He came over, looking to all the world like he was admiring the sleeping baby in the pram, and he said with a great big smile on his face that he'd heard my "retard sister" had died.'

Andrés flinched.

'He used that cruel, nasty, *foul* language against a woman whose only crime had been to love him,' Gabrielle continued, angrily impassioned, 'and then he looked at Lucas, his own flesh and blood, and said that my son looked very peaceful and that it would be a real shame if someone opened their fat mouth and had him taken away.'

Knowing there was a real chance he was going to erupt with the fury her words had triggered in him, Andrés snatched at one part of her sentence to focus his attention on. 'When he said, "my son", who was he referring to? You or him?'

'Me. He must have been keeping tabs on us because he knew I was passing myself as Lucas's mother.'

He had to grit his teeth to ask the next question. 'Have you seen him since?'

'No, but since then I've kept tabs on *him*, and I get the feeling he's been avoiding Monte Cleure since Catalina came to the throne, probably because of all the changes she's making. He couldn't have been invited to her party as he was hosting a shooting weekend at his English estate that weekend. That's how I knew it was safe to go with you.'

'So he's English?'

'I never said that.'

'But he has an English estate that he holds shooting weekends at so will be easy to find.'

'Don't you *dare*,' she said, lifting her face from his chest to look up at him with horror.

'I can deal with this for you,' he said tightly, holding onto his temper by a thread, *only* holding onto it because even amidst the rage flowing through his veins he knew the person he wanted to direct all the rage at wasn't the beautiful woman imploring him with her eyes. 'Give me his name.'

'No.'

'The man is a bully. I have dealt with many bullies in my time.'

'No! You can't. Please, leave things be. I don't want any more of his money and I will not risk Lucas for anything. It would kill me to lose him, so please, please promise you won't do or say anything or say anything or have any contact with that man, *please*.'

So many emotions were contained in those beautiful dark brown eyes another blow smashed into his already bruised chest and the fury ebbed to a simmer.

How big a heart could one woman have? Gabrielle could be filled with bitterness for the cards life had dealt her, could resent the child she'd been emotionally blackmailed into raising as her own at the expense of the future she'd planned for herself, but instead, and without an ounce of self-pity, she'd taken her nephew into her heart and loved and protected him as fiercely as if she'd carried him himself.

He'd thought he'd known the night of the party that Gabrielle was a one-off but he'd had no idea of the extent of it.

She was incredible.

Palming her cheek, he brought his face down to hers, close enough to catch the faint trace of her scent... *Dios*, that scent intoxicated him. It was the scent that had underlined the perfume she'd worn that night, the sweet, unique scent of Gabrielle.

Staring intently into her eyes, he said, 'It took a lot for you to put your trust in me and share what you did, and I will do nothing to abuse it.'

Her chest and shoulders rose and then she dealt another blow to his heart by attempting to smile. 'What I told you about my mother… please don't think she was a bad mother,' she whispered, her eyes once again pleading. 'She wasn't. It's just that my father's death came as a huge shock to her. They were devoted to each other.'

'And a shock to you too, I would imagine,' he pointed out softly.

'Of course it did but I had Romeo to lean on and he had me.'

You were ten, he resisted from saying.

Gabrielle was an emotionally intelligent woman. If she'd forgiven her mother for falling apart when she needed her most then who was he to criticise?

'You'll see when you meet her,' she said. 'She's a very sweet and loving woman, and she's a brilliant grandmother to Lucas, and she'll be a brilliant grandmother to our baby too.'

Our baby.

Two words to make his guts clench…but not as tightly as they'd done a day ago. Not when his gaze was locked on the dark chocolate swirls of Gabrielle's heavenly eyes and those pillowy lips, so ripe for kissing, were moving ever closer to his…

Or was it his lips moving closer to hers?

Dios, how was it possible to ache so badly for someone? Was it because she was carrying his child that he felt so many damned feelings for this woman? That she touched him in a way no one had ever done before?

But the ache for her had started long ago...

Gabrielle felt purged. For the first time since bringing Lucas home, she'd shared the sacrifice her beautiful sister had made for the love of her child, and sharing it had been cathartic. Necessity meant Eloise's love for her son had to be hidden from the world, a secret kept between the three surviving Bretons and the man who didn't want him, a secret kept tightly, the circumstances of his birth never discussed even amongst themselves. And she'd shared too, the one secret she'd kept entirely to herself, deciding it was better her family didn't know because of the hurt it would cause them—the threat The Bastard had made to her. She'd shared it with the man who'd fathered her own child, a man she knew would never reject the life growing inside her, and as she gazed at Andrés, her senses opened up to him like the petals of a flower opening to the sun and she found herself falling into the eyes that had hypnotised her from the very first look.

Their faces were so close she could see the individual bristles of his thick beard, fill her lungs with the divine scent she'd gone to bed every night since their night together playing like a phantom into her airwaves. The sensitive tips of her breasts were barely a whisper away from touching the hard chest she'd been crushed against for comfort only minutes before, and now she could feel them stir in a tingle of anticipation and need, desire awakening and trickling with a steady relentlessness through her veins.

Their lips brushed in the lightest of caresses. The fingers pressed against her cheek tightened.

Her senses filling with the heat of Andrés's breath, she closed her eyes…

The unexpected loud ring of a phone cut through the air.

Eyes flew open and locked back together.

The phone continued to ring.

An instant later, they pulled apart, Gabrielle's heart hammering so loudly it was a drum in her ears.

It frightened her how much she wanted him. Terrified her how comforting it had been to just…*submit* herself and let him give her the comfort she hadn't even known she needed until he'd held her so tightly.

And it frightened her to see the hunger in his eyes. Frightened her because it fed her own.

Andrés took a visible deep breath before pulling the phone from his back pocket. When he saw who the caller was, he came back to life with a curse.

Eyes on Gabrielle, he put it to his ear. 'I told you not to disturb me unless it was life or death.'

His face darkened as he listened to the caller but then something changed, his eyes narrowing. 'Hold on,' he said curtly before covering the mouthpiece and asking Gabrielle, 'When is your mother bringing Lucas back?'

'Tuesday.'

He nodded and spoke again to the caller. 'Co-ordinate with the captain and get the helicopter to me.'

Disconnecting the call, he rubbed the back of his neck and breathed deeply through his nose before meeting her stare. 'We're going to Japan.'

Thrown by the *we*, she stared at him without comprehension.

'The deal I told you about is hanging by a thread,' he explained tersely. 'I need to be there but I also need to be here with you. I cannot magic myself into two places so you will have to come with me.'

It took a good few moments to realise he was serious. 'I can't. I'm working tomorrow, and—'

'Gabrielle, you are having my child. You will never have to work again.'

Her mouth fell open.

'We need to talk seriously about our future

and how we're going to play things, but whatever it holds for you and me, you are the mother of my child and that means your life changes as of now.'

She shook her head in disbelief. 'I'm only weeks pregnant. *Anything* could happen.'

'Yes,' he agreed. 'Anything could happen but that doesn't mean it will, and I will not have you spending the pregnancy living in a cramped apartment when I can provide you with the home of your dreams and everything you need. We have a lot to discuss, *ma belle*, and with Lucas safe with your mother, now is the perfect opportunity to discuss them.'

'I can't just fly to the other side of the world on a whim!'

'Why not?' he challenged.

'Because…' She closed her eyes and took a deep breath. 'You're asking me to trust that when I lose my job—and I guarantee that flying to Japan with you instead of turning up to work will be considered gross misconduct—that you'll… Andrés, it's hard enough making ends meet as it is. I can't afford to miss my mortgage payments.'

Warm hands captured her cheeks.

Opening her eyes she found herself trapped again in Andrés's black stare. 'You trusted me with the truth about Lucas,' he said, his voice

containing the same intensity as his eyes. 'Trust
that I am not Lucas's father and that when I give
my word, I never go back on it. Come to Japan
with me, *ma belle*. I swear you will not suffer
for it. You will never suffer any form of depri-
vation again.'

Gabrielle had never flown before, not by helicopter or plane, so to use both modes of trans-
port within an hour of each other blew her mind.
It blew it almost as much as agreeing to go to
Japan with him.

Within two hours of Andrés receiving the
call, they'd been helicoptered off his yacht,
flown to his apartment, driven to her apartment
to get her passport and an overnight bag she
rammed the first items of clothing to hand in,
driven back to his apartment, then helicoptered
to an airport in Barcelona where they bypassed
what she assumed would be the usual security
checks at an airport to be ushered onto a plane
so luxurious she actually wondered if she'd
fallen into a dream. Only the butterflies in her
stomach, fluttering their wings in time to the
beats of her heart, convinced her this was real.

That and Andrés's cologne.

While she'd been chauffeured to her apartment, he'd showered and changed into a business suit. She'd been stuck in confined spaces

with him smelling good enough to eat ever since, and now she was destined to spend twelve hours with him confined in a space with no escape.

It should not be a thought that sent thrills racing through her veins, just as her lips shouldn't still tingle from that brief caress and just as her stare shouldn't be locked on his face watching every second of the call he'd been on since they arrived at the airfield and which hadn't let up even when he sank onto the plush leather seat opposite hers. The concentration lines on his forehead and the polite curtness of his tone reminded her of how big a deal this deal was to him. One of the biggest deals of his life...

He should have flown to Japan yesterday to deal with it. Instead he'd come to her.

He could have taken his suspicions about Lucas to the authorities. Instead he'd come to her.

Instead of concentrating fully on his important call, his stare kept locking onto hers.

As the plane taxied down the runway, her heart swelled with an emotion so powerful that for a moment she couldn't breathe, and she closed her eyes, trying desperately to swallow it all away.

Andrés watched Gabrielle close her eyes and

struggle for breath, and abruptly ended the call with his finance director.

How could he concentrate on business when the most beautiful woman in the world was directly in his line of sight and the thrills from the connection of their lips were still as vivid as if it had happened only moments ago?

Dios, he could still taste her breath. He breathed it in with every inhalation.

Her chest rose, breasts straining beneath the fabric of her dress and, even as awareness strained his every sinew, he had the sense to remember this was her first time on a plane.

Switching seats to the one beside her, he took hold of her hand and held it tightly.

Her eyes flew back open.

Leaning into her, he said, 'You have *nothing* to be frightened of. Pilots are some of the most highly trained professionals out there. You are safer on a plane than you are on the roads.'

Something flickered on her face, something that set a jolt of pure emotion into his heart.

He'd had no idea hearts could bruise so easily. The story about her sister had been close to unbearable to hear but the bruises had all come from the blows of Gabrielle's tears. Now, each beat, he felt it, like he'd never done before. Just to look at her bruised him in ways he could never explain.

Just to look at her was to want her.

Gabrielle had become so lost in the black depths of Andrés's eyes that she didn't even notice they'd taken off until her stomach dipped from the plane, much like the dips to her stomach he induced.

His phone had saved them before. Saved her.

There was nothing to save her now from the lips she'd dreamed about every night since their one night together closing in on her.

As hard as she'd tried these last weeks to lock Andrés and the joy they'd discovered in each other's arms into her memory box, it had been impossible and after the whirlwind of the last twenty-four hours, she felt like she was walking on quicksand, the body that had clung to the joy fighting with the brain that knew all the feelings sweeping and clinging to that body were dangerous…

But when their lips met, the quicksand deepened and she was helpless to do anything but sink into it.

CHAPTER TWELVE

ANDRÉS LED GABRIELLE into the plane's bedroom, far beyond caring what was happening in Japan or anywhere. He was beyond thinking.

From the burning daze in her eyes, she was gripped by the same fever.

As soon as the door closed behind them, their mouths and limbs fused back together in one ravenous moan. Hungry lips parted, tongues plunging and exploring, and in no time at all Gabrielle's legs were wrapped around his waist and he was carrying her to the bed.

Dios, he'd dreamed of this for so long.

All those nights, Gabrielle and the night they'd shared together haunting him.

Clothes were stripped and flung without care.

Both fully naked, Gabrielle on her back, chest rising and falling rapidly, cheeks flushed…he soaked in every inch, taking in the changes pregnancy had already made, changes that would be imperceptible to anyone else.

Desire as strong as he'd ever felt gripped him at the same time his chest tightened to a sharp point. That was his baby developing in her softly rounded stomach. The swelling of her breasts was the pregnancy preparing her body for the gift of life.

She'd never looked more beautiful.

Climbing between her legs, he pushed her thighs back and kissed her with a savagery she matched with her own.

She writhed against him, nails scraping over his back as she groped for his buttocks, her breaths hot and ragged, urging his possession.

His arousal guiding itself to the heat of her femininity, he drove into her.

Dios, he came *this* close to losing it with that first thrust.

He'd thought he'd remembered the intensity of the brief pleasure of being inside Gabrielle completely bare but this was something else.

Gabrielle had lost herself to the quicksand. Every cell and nerve ending burned at the feel of Andrés's huge body covering her and possessing her.

If this was madness then she gave herself to it willingly, throwing off the shackles of her fears for the hedonistic connection that felt as necessary as breathing.

Gabrielle's moans of pleasure fell like nectar into Andrés's ears and fed the fever gripping him. This went beyond *everything* and he was having to fight to hold on, fighting and fighting until her moans shallowed and he felt the thickening around him. Thrusting himself so deep inside her he didn't know where he ended and she began, he shouted out her name and climaxed with enough force to shatter himself into atoms.

Tokyo was the most fascinating place Gabrielle could have dreamed of, and considering she was completely thrown by being in a completely different time zone, everything happening to her felt much like a waking dream. It had done since she'd fallen back under Andrés's spell on his plane.

They'd spent the whole flight in that bed. All talk about their future, the very reason for her accompanying him, had been forgotten as they'd made love, dozed, made love and dozed until time had run out.

Andrés had been locked in perpetual meetings to thrash out the deal's stumbling blocks ever since.

While he'd tried to salvage the deal that meant so much to him, Gabrielle toured Tokyo's streets with the French-speaking guide he'd arranged to keep her company and act as translator, with the thrums of their lovemaking beating strongly inside her.

She couldn't get over how clean the city was. She'd thought Monte Cleure was clean but here it was so spotless it all looked brand new. In complete contrast to the seemingly chaotic roads they'd travelled to their hotel on, the pedestrian areas were sprawling and orderly, the high-rises dominating the skyline making her feel buffeted and safe.

Everything about Tokyo seemed busy, busy, busy but she never felt that she had to rush. An air of politeness pervaded the city and she wished she had more time to spend here and explore. If Andrés pulled the deal off then he would become a frequent visitor to the city.

Who would he bring with him the next time he came?

It was a thought she quickly pushed aside. They were having a baby together; their lives would always be entwined, but she wasn't foolish enough to expect anything more, not with the memory of her sister's desolation at The Bastard's cruel treatment so fresh in her mind.

Eloise's pure heart had fallen madly in love and it had been smashed into pieces.

Andrés would never treat Gabrielle the way Eloise had been treated but that didn't mean she shouldn't tread carefully with him. Treading on quicksand with lust when that lust would come to a natural end was one thing. Planning a future where their lives were entwined around their child was another thing.

Imagining a future, a real future, with a man who didn't do future was for fools.

After two backbreaking days, the deal was ninety per cent assured.

Confident his team could take it from there,

Andrés took Gabrielle to one of Tokyo's hidden gems, a Kaiseki restaurant set in a quiet residential area.

Their table overlooked a tranquil secret garden, an abundance of sweet-scented flowers in full bloom. Gabrielle outshone its beauty.

Ravishing in a pretty black kimono-style dress with red lilies embroidered onto it that she'd bought earlier, one look had been enough to steal his breath, just as she'd stolen it that first night.

Just as she did every time he looked at her.

'What time do we have to leave?' she asked, attempting to grip a matsutake mushroom with her chopsticks. Andrés had offered to ask for cutlery but, determined to master it, she'd refused.

To his deep regret, this was the first meal other than breakfast they'd been able to share together. Negotiations over the deal had been more fraught than even he'd anticipated, the cultural differences as difficult to navigate as the main business issues. He'd returned to the hotel both nights mentally drained but still intending to discuss the issues he'd insisted Gabrielle accompany him here to discuss, only to take one look at her and find all thoughts escaping his mind.

'Early in the morning. With the time difference and the flight times, we'll be back in Monte Cleure with time for you to rest before your mother brings Lucas home.'

She shook her head. 'How do you cope with it all? I've only just got over the flight over and adjusted to being in a different time zone, and now we have to go back. You do this kind of travelling constantly. Doesn't it exhaust you?'

'I can sleep anywhere and never suffered from jet lag so it's never been an issue for me,' he dismissed with a shrug. 'But I'm going to make changes to my schedule now that we're having a baby. All this travelling across continents isn't right with a child. Children need stability.'

Her thoughtful gaze settled on him. 'If our baby's raised with a father who spends a great deal of time travelling then that will be his or her normal. That will be stable.'

'Not in the way I want and it is for this reason that I think we should live together.'

Andrés didn't know who was more disarmed at his choice of words, himself who hadn't meant for it to come out like that, or Gabrielle who almost choked on a bonito flake.

Luckily a drink of water was enough for her to catch her breath, and he explained his thinking before his mis-choice of words could root. 'I grew up with parents who hated the sight of each other but being together as a family was important to me. Like you, I only want what's best for our child, and I want them to grow up knowing that if they wake in the night with a terror, that their mother and father are both there for them, and I think the best way of doing that is if I buy a property to use as our main home where we can each have our own wing and lead our own lives but still be under the same roof.'

He watched her intelligent eyes process this.

'You can choose where we live. It can be Monte Cleure if you wish. Wherever you choose, this arrangement will allow us both to keep our independence and once this…' He had to swallow a sudden lump in his throat. '…thing between us fades away, we will be in a position to parent as friends, if not lovers.' His eyes glittered as he added, 'I will be honest with you, Gabrielle, *ma belle*, I am in no hurry for that to happen. What we have between us is pretty damn incredible.'

Gabrielle's heart was beating fast, and she drank some more of her iced water in an attempt to calm herself.

This *thing*.

What a horrible way to describe something so beautiful.

But that was Andrés, she accepted painfully.

He did not do emotional commitment to anyone that was not blood.

It was nothing she didn't already know. More importantly, it was nothing she didn't want for herself. When their sexual relationship ended, her heart would be perfectly intact.

For all her internal reasoning, it took effort to make her voice temperate. 'I had both my parents for the first ten years of my life and I will be for ever grateful for that, but if they'd never lived together, that would have been my normal and I wouldn't have known any different.'

'I want to be there, Gabrielle. Why do you think I've been so intent *not* to have children? It's because I've always known how I would feel. The thought of my child growing up under a different roof to me and living with a man who is not me is intolerable.'

'I can put your mind at rest on the second part. I have no intention of living with anyone.'

His black eyes glimmered. 'I'm not *anyone*. I'm the father of your child.'

'And you're not proposing that I live with you in that way, but I don't imagine many other people will understand it. What do you think will happen if Lucas's father learns about us?'

'I can protect you both from that man.'

'Maybe you can, I don't know, but either way, this...' She scrambled to put her thoughts into order. 'It's a good, logical idea.' She had to admit that. In many ways it was the perfect solution for two people who shied away from real relationships. 'But I have Lucas to think of, and not just because of his father. He's used to it being just the two of us. He needs to get to know you, and you need to get to know him, and until I know he's comfortable with you I can't even entertain the idea of us sharing a house.'

'I will get to know him and work on building his trust.'

'That's great but there has to be boundaries. He can't know that you and I are lovers, and if all goes well with the two of you and we get that house you talked about, you can't bring women to it. That part of your life will have to be separate. I will not have him confused or upset for anything. He's been through too much as it is.'

He raised his wine glass. 'I can accept those terms.'

Gabrielle clinked her grape Ramune to it, managing a tight smile, proud that she'd been able to give her conditions without her voice cracking.

This really was the perfect solution. Other than Lucas's emotional security, there was not one good reason to dislike it, not when it gave them both everything they needed and, more importantly, provided the children with the stability that all children deserved, and she couldn't understand why her stomach was twisting so tightly.

Andrés thanked the waitress who'd appeared to clear their table in preparation for the next course, and drank the last of his wine.

Gabrielle had agreed—in a roundabout way—to his eminently sensible proposal. Her only reservations were also eminently sensible. He should be delighted, thrilled that he'd judged correctly that the headiness of the chemistry they currently shared wouldn't cloud her thinking and compel her to ask for more than he wanted to give.

He should be feeling euphoric that they'd organised everything so neatly, not feeling flattened.

Gabrielle had assumed Andrés's Spanish home would be palatial. She'd severely underestimated. There, in the heart of the city, set back off a wide road with wide pavements lined with orange trees, a beautiful three storey townhouse that dominated the entire area.

If she was overawed, she thought Lucas's eyes were at risk of popping out.

Where the architecture of the house had a gothic feel, the interior was sleek and modern with distinctive Spanish touches. Three living rooms. *Three.* Two dining rooms. *Two dining rooms!* A study that also doubled as a library. A games room. A cinema room. All except the latter with high, frescoed ceilings and late afternoon light pouring in at all angles. Each bedroom had its own adjoining bathroom.

Then there was the grounds, a perfect oasis of beauty surrounded by a perimeter of huge trees that gave the illusion of being in the middle of nowhere.

They toured it all, Lucas clutching her hand, even more intimidated than he'd been when they'd spent the day in Andrés's apartment last weekend.

For a month they'd been working on getting Lucas comfortable with Andrés. This hadn't been helped by the amount of travelling Andrés had done, their time together coming in fits and spurts. His intention was that by the time the baby came, he'd have moved his head offices to wherever she decided they would set up home together and be under the same roof as her at least eighty per cent of the time. One place he'd asked her to consider was Seville, the city he called home, and so she'd agreed to bring Lucas for a weekend there. Andrés had cleared his entire diary for them, and invited his family over, including his godsons in the hope that seeing other children comfortable with him would help Lucas learn he wasn't a bogeyman.

But it wasn't just the travelling that had stopped Andrés and Lucas from bonding. The simple truth was Lucas distrusted him, and no amount of toys as bribes or rides in a helicopter could get him to view Andrés with anything less than suspicion. As a result, Gabrielle had refused Andrés's offer of renting a home for them until she deemed the time right for him to buy them the house he'd spoken of. His presence in their life had unsettled her little boy enough without ripping him from the cosy apartment that had been their home his entire life, the deposit for it paid with the last of The Bastard's hush money.

Her brother, spectacularly useless at emotional stuff but excellent with practical stuff, had insisted on paying the small mortgage until she'd been in a position to go out to work; his way of playing his part, and she intended to offer it to him when she moved out.

She still couldn't get over having the luxury of being able to let it out rent free. Without her knowledge, Andrés had paid the mortgage off. For the first time in her life, Gabrielle had money to burn, all thanks to Andrés and the money he'd deposited into her account, also without her knowledge. She'd begged her col-

leagues' forgiveness for skipping to Japan and
parted on good terms with them, her mother
had accepted the situation with a stoic grace,
and for the first time in almost five years, the
future she'd once wanted for herself looked possible. More than once, Andrés had mentioned
her doing the degree she'd always wanted.

Really, she should be buzzing that her future
was brighter than she'd ever imagined it could
be, but for a reason she couldn't discern, a ker-
nel of fear still beat in her chest.

She would wait until the baby had been born
before making any decisions about her personal
future. As it was, there was too much in her
head to think beyond the next day. Everything
in her head was wrapped around Andrés and it
frightened her how completely he occupied her
mind. It frightened her even more how much
she missed him when he was away.

Those nights in Japan had spoilt her because
she'd never known nights could be lonely.

She'd have to get used to lonely nights per-
manently once he'd bored of her, a thought she
steadfastly refused to allow to set in, and as the
sun went down on her first night in Seville and
her exhausted child fell asleep in his ice-cream,
her pulse quickened to think that after five days
of no physical contact, they could be together.

'Let me carry him up,' Andrés said, carefully lifting Lucas from his seat.

He opened his eyes, and immediately looked over Andrés's shoulder for her, but instead of reaching for her when his eyes found her, rested his head back on Andrés and relaxed.

Only once Andrés had laid him on the king-size bed of the room he'd been appointed for the weekend, did their eyes meet in silent wonder at this huge leap in progress.

'I'm going to take a shower and get to bed myself,' Andrés said, throwing her completely.

'Oh. Okay,' she said, simply because she couldn't think of anything else to say.

A faint smile played on his lips. 'Goodnight, Lucas. Sweet dreams.'

He slipped out of the room leaving Gabrielle bewildered and disconcerted that he didn't wish her a goodnight too.

The staff having already unpacked their possessions for them, it was for once an easy matter to get her usually wriggling child into his pyjamas. Lucas was simply too exhausted from the lateness of the hour, the travelling and excitement of the day to be anything other than compliant, no energy to even wriggle at the sight of the toothbrush aiming for his mouth.

He was asleep before she'd read two pages to him.

Kissing his forehead, she whispered, 'I love you,' before creeping out of his room and into her own adjoining one.

Oh, well, she thought moodily as she closed the door, if Andrés was going to bed then she might as well too. And at least her room was fit for a princess and had a television because she didn't feel in the least bit sleepy.

And at least she had her own beautiful bathroom, and when she stood under the powerful shower head she tried not to let the panic nibbling at her heart take root, only to find that actively trying not to let the panic take root had the opposite effect.

Was he boring of her *already*? Was that really possible when he called her every night? When he pulled her into his arms the second they were alone, which admittedly wasn't enough for either of their liking.

The emotions rising in her chest threatening to erupt, she wrestled her pyjama shorts and vest top on, and brushed her teeth harder than she'd ever done before stomping back into the bedroom…

Andrés was in her bed.

Her mouth fell open. 'What are you doing?'

He threw the bedsheets off him. He was naked, and fully erect. 'Thinking about you.'

'But…' She could hardly think let alone speak

under the weight of her relief. 'I thought you were going to bed.'

His eyes gleamed wickedly. 'I didn't say whose bed I was going to.' He gripped his arousal. 'Going to join me?'

Unconsciously, she cupped her breast, even as she shook her head. 'I...' She swallowed the moisture that had flooded her mouth. 'I can't.'

He nodded at the tablet on the bedside table. 'Turn that on.'

'What?'

'It's a monitor. If he wakes, it will alert you.'

She pressed the biggest of the buttons. Immediately the screen filled with an image of Lucas sleeping.

'Touch the screen.'

She did so. The screen went blank.

'Now it is set to sound activation.' His voice thickened and his movements over his excitement strengthened. 'Take your clothes off.'

Now fully locked in the sexual haze Andrés was exuding, Gabrielle pulled her vest top up and over her head.

He groaned.

A surge of heady power rushed through her at the effect she was having on him, and she stepped back. Cupping a breast and rubbing a thumb over the erect nipple, she dipped her other hand beneath the band of her pyjama shorts and touched the core of her own arousal.

'Let me see,' he begged.

Now it was her turn to smile wickedly. Squeezing her breast, she continued to pleasure herself, all the while relishing and feeding off the effect it was having on him.

'Do you do that to yourself at night when you're alone?' he whispered.

She answered with a lascivious smile and pulled her shorts down.

'I do,' he said hoarsely, eyes glazed, his hand now a blur, the tip of his excitement glistening. 'Every night when I get into my lonely bed, I close my eyes and think of you naked. I imagine touching you and being inside you…it is all I think about.'

He crooked a finger at her.

The burn of desire now so strong she could hardly walk, her legs obeyed his wordless command.

In seconds he had her flat on her back.

Seconds later he was inside her and the burn blazed into a flame that scorched them both.

Early dawn light was filtering through the curtains when, with a strangled moan, Andrés climaxed.

For the longest time they did nothing but lie

there, holding each other tightly, hearts beating in rhythm as they caught their breath.

How was it possible for his desire for Gabrielle to keep strengthening the way it did?

He'd never felt such reluctance to leave a bed before.

He gave Gabrielle one last kiss and pulled the sheets off him.

He was already counting the hours down until they would be together again.

Gabrielle watched Andrés slip silently out of the bedroom and closed her eyes in an effort to control the emotions swelling in her chest.

The bed already felt empty without him.

She already felt empty without him.

CHAPTER THIRTEEN

ANDRÉS FELT A tug on his shorts and looked down to find Lucas gazing up at him.

'Andrés, can I go in the pool with Raul?'

'Have you asked your mummy?'

He shook his head.

'Then we should go and ask her.'

Lucas slipped his hand into Andrés's.

Trying hard not to show his shock at this unsolicited trusting gesture, he put his beer on the table and walked across the lawn to where Gabrielle and Sophia were sprawled out on two of the many sun loungers spread around the pool, deep in conversation.

Gabrielle wasn't quick enough to hide her surprise at seeing Lucas's hand in Andrés's.

Was that good surprise or bad surprise? He couldn't judge. There was something about Gabrielle's mood that day that struck him as off. Not that *she* was being off. No, it wasn't that, more a melancholy? No, not that either. He couldn't think what the little glimpses into the distance as if she were lost in thought and then the blink back to the present and the usual smile lifting on her face he kept catching meant.

'Lucas wants to go for a swim,' he told her.

She looked at her son. 'Okay, but put your T-shirt back on.'

'But…'

'No arguing. You'll burn your shoulders. Where did you put your armbands?'

He ran off to get them.

Gabrielle's gaze turned to Andrés. 'Looks like you're starting to win him over,' she murmured.

He raised his eyebrows and crossed his fingers.

She grinned but before she could say anything further, Lucas came charging back with the armbands, closely followed by Andrés's godson Raul who had a unicorn rubber ring around his waist. The two boys being a similar age had hit it off in the way only small children could, becoming instant best friends.

Lucas gave the armbands to Andrés to put on for him. 'Will you come in too?' he asked shyly.

He couldn't have been more moved if the boy had embraced him.

Swallowing, he tapped the boy's snub little nose. 'Sure. But no splashing me.'

Minutes later shrieks of laughter filled the pool area as the two small boys mercilessly splashed water over Andrés, who splashed them back with equal ruthlessness. Gabrielle watched it all with a huge smile on her face and a huge fist in her heart.

Bringing him to Seville and the relaxed atmosphere of it all was having the effect they'd both hoped for and now, finally, she could see the Andrés effect working its magic on her son.

Which meant that soon he would broach the subject of them all moving in together as one big family in two separate wings.

'Something on your mind?'

Sophia's voice broke through her thoughts.

Bringing her smile back, glad she'd put her sunglasses on, she said, 'Just thinking how great it is to see Lucas having fun.'

'Andrés has always been good with children.'

This was the first time Sophia had mentioned her brother since they'd sat down together twenty minutes ago. Instead, their chat had been Gabrielle filling her in on the party, a valiant attempt made to remember the names of the people they'd been sat at the table with, and not making it sound as if she'd been so wrapped up in Sophia's brother that she'd forgotten to beg an introduction to the Queen she idolised and completely failed to soak in the full magic of the evening.

She'd been wrapped in an entirely different magic. She was still wrapped in it, had enveloped herself so tightly in it that, despite her efforts to kid herself that Andrés's magic only reached her loins, the desolation she'd felt when he'd left her bed that morning proved she was becoming vulnerable.

One day he would leave her bed for good. She

had to be prepared for that, especially now that Lucas was taking him into his heart.

'You know, I hoped this would happen.'

Broken out of yet another reverie, Gabrielle again forced her attention to Sophia. 'Hoped what?'

'That you and Andrés would get together.'

'It isn't like… Hold on, did you say you *hoped* we would get together?'

Sophia smiled. 'My brother has been a selfish asshole for too long. Do you know this is the first time he's had the whole family over since he bought this place? He needs a woman like you, someone straight talking and who will call him out when he needs it, not those insipid women who cling to his every word and bore him in seconds. It's easy to say you're never going to marry or settle down when you only involve yourself with women you can picture yourself breaking up with.'

Stunned, her heart beating fast—too fast—something finally became clear. 'You faked your sickness.'

'I did,' Sophia admitted without an ounce of shame. 'You were just so unimpressed with him, it was hilarious, *and* you amused him, I saw it, and I saw the look you gave each other. I'm a big believer in trusting my gut—remind me to tell you how I met my husband—and my gut was telling me loud and clear that you had the potential to be perfect for him. You can say thank you to my gut when his ring's on your finger.'

Before Gabrielle could tell Sophia that was never going to happen, the Spanish woman's voice dropped. 'Uh oh, our parents have arrived. Andrés has told you about them?'

'Only that they have a toxic marriage.'

'He thinks it's toxic. I've come to think it's funny. It's like getting a ringside seat to the Punch and Judy show for free, but without the violence. Come on, I'll introduce you to them.'

The party Andrés had organised intending it to be a lunchtime affair spread into the evening. His staff were as excellent and efficient as always, bringing out an endless supply of food and ensuring the garden bar was always fully stocked. After an especially vigorous game of football in which Andrés, Lucas, Raul and Gabrielle made a team against his father, Mateo his other godson, Mateo's father and Sophia's husband, and thrashed them eight nil—Gabrielle made a surprisingly effective goalkeeper—the happy, exhausted children were sent to bed in Lucas's room and the champagne was opened.

Music piped through the garden speakers, they pulled chairs into an informal circle and everything was great, the most fun he'd had with his family since he could remember, and then his parents, who'd kept their sniping at each other down to pointed barbs and muttered insults, spoiled the relaxed atmosphere by having a stand-up blazing row that ended with his mother storming inside and his father rolling his eyes at anyone who would look at him.

A hand covered his. 'Are you okay?'

He locked onto Gabrielle's eyes and felt much of the poison witnessing that charade had induced drain away. 'I'm good.'

Her lips curved in sympathy. 'That was quite the performance.'

'That is one way to describe it.'

'It's strange how Sophia finds their behaviour funny but you find it toxic.'

'She finds it funny now but she hated it as much as I did when we were kids.'

'Maybe her own marriage gave her a change of perspective.'

He grunted.

'Have to admit, I'm leaning to the Sophia side.'

A black eyebrow shot up. Gabrielle shrugged. Having observed his parents together that day, she understood where Andrés was coming from but as an outsider, she didn't think it was all bad. 'The impression I get is that they seem very close. Maybe arguing is their language with each other. Everyone else just seems to roll with it.' She shrugged again. 'I don't know,

I've only just met them, and as we're speaking of your family, you never told me Sophia faked her illness for the party.' She strove to keep her voice casual as she said this.

The more she'd thought about it, the more Gabrielle thought she should have guessed, but then how could she have? Who faked illness to shoehorn a stranger to take your place at a royal party? To Gabrielle, Sophia had been just another rich woman used to the world revolving around her, albeit an unusually nice one.

Now she thought she understood Sophia's thinking. Sophia was happily married. Her brother had had a succession of affairs with the same breed of women, none of whom made him happy because he'd chosen those women deliberately. She'd spotted her chance to foist someone different on him, someone who, in her words, had the *potential to be perfect for him*, and had taken it.

It was those words… Every time she thought of them, the weight in her stomach grew.

There was a flash of surprise and then comprehension and a low chuckle. 'She gave you a straight answer on that?'

'Yes.'

'That's more than I got when I confronted her. By the time we left for the palace I knew but she refused to admit it outright. My sister is a law unto herself.' His black eyes gleamed. 'You know she will take credit for the baby when we tell them?' Which would have to be soon as it wouldn't be long before Gabrielle was visibly showing. They'd agreed to wait until after the weekend before sharing the news with his family.

From the corner of his eyes, Andrés spotted his mother come back outside. Usually this would not be something he thought twice about but with Gabrielle's observations about his parents still fresh, he turned to watch her. It was only because he was actively watching that he noticed her trail her fingers over the back of his father's neck as she retook her seat next to him. If he hadn't been observing them so closely, he would have missed his father reach back to squeeze her hand.

The hairs on Andrés's arm lifted.

He closed his eyes. When he reopened them, he noticed his mother had already started an animated conversation with one of his cousins but that her right foot was pressed against his father's left foot.

'Andrés?'

His heart began to pound.

'Andrés?'

Slowly turning his head, he met Gabrielle's concerned stare and suddenly found it impossible to look away. The thoughts churning in his head were as impossible to comprehend as the emotions smashing into his chest.

Andrés had always kept his head down when his parents argued, normally escaping to another room until the storm fully passed, not wanting to be forced to see their hatred for each other as well as hear it. It felt like he'd done that for his entire life.

How many other small intimacies had he missed over the years? And as he wondered this, the realisation came that although he'd lived with them, he hadn't lived their marriage. He'd never worked the hours the two of them had during his childhood and still not earned enough to meet the bills.

Was it any wonder they'd taken the stress and exhaustion out on each other?

The stress from their lives had gone and now they liked to bicker and argue for fun or out of habit, but whatever their reason...

So what?

In his loathing of the toxic nature of their marriage, he'd missed the love that underpinned it and was their marriage's foundation.

Sophia had been raised in the same household. She hadn't replicated their marriage. Sophia was happy.

Gazing into the eyes of the bravest, fiercest, sexiest woman in the world, eyes containing an ocean of emotions directed at *him*, his own future suddenly became clear.

'When will we see Andrés again?' Lucas asked as she went to switch his light off.

'Soon.'

'Can we go for another sleepover at his house?'

'I'm sure that can be arranged.'

'Will Raul be there?'

'I don't know. We can ask. Now go to sleep.'

After another kiss to his forehead, she trundled back to the living area of her apartment that, after the glorious weekend in Seville, felt claustrophobic.

Or maybe it was her thoughts making her feel that way.

No sooner had she curled on her sofa than her phone rang.

She closed her eyes before answering it. Andrés had the uncanny ability to know exactly when the right time to call was.

Before Seville, she'd lived for his calls. In the three days since he'd dropped her home, she'd come to dread them, dreaded the direction the conversation would take. His business must be keeping him extra busy because so far he'd failed to mention the home she'd more or less promised to move into with him once he'd won Lucas over. But he would. Soon. She could feel it in her bones.

The quicksand was fastening around her.

She'd felt its weight in Seville when she'd wanted to cry when he'd left her bed, felt it tighten as the miracle they'd been waiting for of Lucas accepting Andrés had come into being, and then start to pull her down with the words of Sophia continually floating in her ear.

You had the potential to be perfect for him.

Being without him after those wonderful days in Seville…

She needed to end things now, before she found herself stuck in the quicksand for ever.

Before she had her heart broken in the way she'd seen a broken heart destroy those she loved so dear.

'Gabrielle, *ma belle*,' he sang once she'd answered. 'How has your day been?'

Trying to inject life into her voice, she filled him in.

Once he'd given the potted highlights of his own day, to which she tried valiantly to make appropriate responses, he said, 'I will be flying back late tomorrow afternoon. Come to the apartment? I'll do dinner. There's much we need to talk about.'

The thump of dread that banged into her chest winded her.

'Bring Lucas with you,' he added. 'I'll get the spare room made up for him.' Loud voices echoed in the background. He muttered a curse before saying, 'I'm sorry but I need to go. I'll have my driver collect you for seven. Goodnight, *ma belle*. Think of me.'

The line disconnected.

Sleep took a long time to come that night.

Andrés entered the London skyscraper that had once been considered an architectural marvel but now looked sad and pathetic in comparison to the Gherkin, the Shard and the like crowding it out of existence, and was escorted to the elevator and up to the fifteenth floor. The elevator too, had seen better days. He briefly wondered if his antipathy to the building was in part caused by his antipathy to its owner.

His escort took him into a large reception room and announced him to one of the receptionists, who made the call.

A door opened and Gregory Jameson appeared, striding towards him with his hand outstretched.

Smiling with his teeth, Andrés shook the hand vigorously and followed him into the office, signing to his bodyguard, who'd spent the past two weeks twiddling his thumbs, to stay in the reception room.

'I have to say, it is an absolute pleasure to meet you,' Gregory said as he took a seat on one of his plush office sofas.

Andrés took the opposite sofa, laid his briefcase flat beside him and hooked an ankle to a thigh. 'Believe me, the pleasure is all mine.'

A secretary bustled in with coffee, pastries and water. Once she'd left, Gregory said, 'So, to business. I understand you want to discuss a proposal that could make us both a heck of a lot of money.'

Andrés picked up a chocolate croissant without bothering to use a plate, and took a huge bite out of it. 'Actually,' he said after swallowing, 'it's a proposal that, if you accept, will protect the wealth you already have.'

Thirty minutes later, Andrés put the pre-prepared and freshly signed documents back into his briefcase and got to his feet. Sweeping the crumbs that had fallen over his suit from the pastries he'd consumed onto the floor, making sure to scatter them in all directions, he extended a hand.

Gregory looked at it much as a lamb conscious of its fate would look at the knife about to slaughter it.

Andrés kept his steely gaze fixed on the spineless coward and his hand extended until Gregory's tremulous fingers reached over.

When Andrés strode out of the office, Gregory was rocking with his closed hand loosely tucked under an armpit debating through the throbbing pain whether what he needed to call for first was a hand doctor or a bucket of ice.

CHAPTER FOURTEEN

IT WAS WITH a pounding heart that Gabrielle entered Andrés's apartment.

'No Lucas?' he asked, swooping in for a quick, hungry kiss which she wasn't quick enough to duck out of the way of and which made her heart both sigh with the pleasure of it and sink to the pit of her stomach to know it was the last real kiss they would share.

She kicked her ballet shoes off and followed him through the reception room and into the main living area. 'I got my mother to babysit.'

His eyes narrowed slightly before he shrugged and lifted a folder from the table. 'Maybe it is for the best. It means we can talk while we eat. The chef is preparing steak for us.'

Carrying the folder into the dining room, he put it on the table next to the place setting with the glass of iced water already poured, then pulled out Gabrielle's chair.

She sat, trying not to look at the surplus place setting with the glass of milk. It made her heart hurt.

Andrés had a large drink of the red wine already poured to accompany his meal, and nodded at the folder. 'Open that.'

Certain it would contain house details, she opened the lip.

'Start with the top document.'

She had to read it three times for it to make sense. Or, rather, for her brain to comprehend what she understood on the first read but which the violent thrashing of her heart pumping hot blood swimming in her head made impossible to digest.

'Gregory has signed away all rights to Lucas,' he explained into the ringing silence. 'I have bought a majority shareholding in his company. If he makes one move out of line then I sell for a loss and destroy him. The country estate he is so proud of is owned by the company, ergo it is now owned by me. I have put a loaded gun to his head but I have left it for you and your family to decide if you want me to pull the trigger.'

She could only stare at him, hardly able to believe her eyes or ears. Hardly able to dare.

'I know you were worried about the consequences of my involvement in this, but once I'd gathered and dissected all the information about him and got my legal team—who are all bound by confidentiality so please don't worry about them—onto it, I knew I could make my move without any penalty to you or to Lucas.' His eyes were shining. 'This has freed you, Gabrielle. He can never do anything to hurt you or your family again.'

It took a long time for her to whisper, 'Why didn't you tell me you were doing this?'

The shine dimmed a fraction but his gaze remained steady. 'I was trying to clear a burden that has laid heavily in you for far too long before I asked you to marry me.'

Gabrielle was almost stunned into silence. 'You… You want to *marry* me?'

'Not only that but I want to adopt Lucas too.'

Now she really was too stunned to respond.

'This is the point where you're supposed to say something.' His tone was teasing but she detected a slight edge to it.

She had to swallow hard to make her weak vocal cords work. 'But we're not going to marry. We're going to move in together and live in separate wings and lead independent lives.'

'I have had a change of perspective about things,' he explained slowly. 'It was the party. My parents' arguing.' He shook his head and drank some more of his wine. 'What you said… it made me look, and for the first time I saw their marriage clearly. Everything they've been through and all the hardships they suffered. Those circumstances…we will never have to go through what they have. Our marriage doesn't have to be like theirs.'

It came to Gabrielle in a flash that he was serious, and as that penetrated she was transported back to the palace when she'd been dancing in his arms, terrified of the feelings sweeping through her, telling herself that she should run.

She *had* run... But she'd run in the wrong direction. She should have run all the way out of the palace.

She'd run only far enough for him to catch her.

Scrambling to her feet, all the dread and fear she'd been carrying inside her leapt up her throat as a loud, *'No.'*

For the beat of a moment Andrés thought he'd misheard her. 'No?'

'No. I don't want to marry you. I'm grateful—so grateful—for what you've done freeing us from that man, but I can't marry you.'

He looked at her carefully, taking in the wildness of her stare.

A pulse throbbed in the side of his head. None of this was going at all as he'd envisaged.

Andrés had returned to Monte Cleure with the same lightness in his chest being with Gabrielle had induced at the palace. The future he'd seen so clearly in Seville had only brightened, the certainty that he was taking the right path, the certainty not just of his feelings but of hers too.

The passion. The tenderness. The emotions he'd glimpsed when she'd looked at him before she could blink them away.

What he hadn't paid attention to was the duller tone of her voice in all their calls since Seville. If he'd not been so intent on his quest to free her from the English monster, he would have paid better attention to it.

And if he'd not been so intent on giving her the document that had freed her, he'd have paid better attention to her closed-off body language when she'd entered his apartment, and her failure to bring Lucas.

'Why not?'

He detected movement in the doorway. Michael bringing their dinner to them.

'Leave us,' he commanded, not taking his eyes off Gabrielle.

The door closed.

Those few seconds of distraction had given her time to compose herself for her tone was a fraction calmer. 'Marriage is unnecessary. We both know that. I appreciate that Lucas has accepted you and that we can move in together, but I think it best we abide by the original agreement and live as individuals with separate living accommodation raising our baby as one. I'm glad you recognise your parents' marriage isn't as toxic as you've always thought but that—'

'Oh, it is,' he interrupted, holding tightly onto the emotions rising like a cobra in his chest. 'Incredibly toxic, and not the kind of marriage I would wish for any child to suffer, but it is their marriage and for whatever reason it works for them. My epiphany, if you can call it that, is understanding that it is *their* marriage. Not mine. Not one you and I would have. We were already committing our lives together as parents but things have—'

Now Gabrielle was the one to interrupt, the panic clawing at her chest scratching deeper with each passing second. 'I'm abiding by our agreement—it's you who's trying to change it. I don't want to get married, so please respect that and let's put an end to this conversation. In fact, I think it best I go home and we discuss all the other issues another time.'

She'd moved only two paces from the table when he said, 'You still haven't given me a reason.'

She closed her eyes and fought for breath. 'I don't have to give you a reason.'

'Agreed, but it would be courteous seeing as you're throwing my proposal back in my face. Your silence about me adopting Lucas is very telling too.'

Something inside her snapped and she spun back around to face him. 'Why are you *being* like this? We had everything arranged and now all this? You don't even *want* to marry me.'

His face darkened. Arms slowly folding across his chest, he said in a silky tone, 'Making assumptions again? You did that when you told me of the pregnancy. You assumed I either wouldn't want you to keep it—you can have no idea how offensive I found that assumption—and assumed I would force DNA tests.'

'Can you blame me for that?' she cried.

'I was honest with you about the circumstances with Susi and they were nothing like our circumstances.' His tone hardened. 'You assumed the worst of me then and you're assuming the worst of me now.'

She took a deep breath, trying her hardest to fight her insides from unravelling. 'Andrés, if it wasn't for the baby, you wouldn't even be entertaining the idea of marriage.'

'Only because without the baby there would be no you and I, but there *is* a baby, and there is a you and I, and there is a little boy crying out for a father.'

Andrés watched the anger ignite in her eyes. 'Don't bring Lucas into this,' she said fiercely.

'Why not when you've spent years hiding behind him?' he sneered.

'Now you're the one being offensive. You know—'

'I know that you were a twenty-three-year-old virgin with no intention of ever forming a serious relationship and you used Lucas's father as a means to justify it.' Pressing his hands on the table, he rose to his feet. 'Those means have now gone. He is no longer a threat to you. There is nothing—*nothing*—to stop you from committing yourself properly to me.'

'Other than I don't want to. You're so damn arrogant, thinking you can spring this on me and that I'll just bow down to your will.'

'If it's arrogance to believe your feelings run as deep as mine do then yes, I'm arrogant. Look me in the eye and tell me you don't have feelings for me,' he demanded. 'Look me in the eye and tell me you're not feeling everything I feel for you.'

She turned her face away.

He slammed his palm onto the table. 'God in heaven, Gabrielle, what are you so frightened of? Or are you just being blind? Don't you get it? There hasn't been anyone else for me since the moment you pulled my car over, now look me in the eyes and tell me you're not in love with me. If you can do that, then I will let you go and never mention marriage again.'

Gabrielle's stomach was rolling so violently

she feared she'd be sick, images flashing, her distraught sister on the floor of the bathroom, her mother turning her pillow sodden with tears, all the damage, so much damage, that came when hearts were broken into pieces.

It took all the strength she possessed to step back to the table and meet his stare.

She could hardly make her throat move let alone hold his stare to truthfully croak, 'I left Lucas at home tonight because I was going to tell you that *this thing* between us…' Her throat caught. 'Is over.'

The clenching of his jaw was the only hint of emotion to pass his face.

And then he smiled cruelly. 'That is not what I asked of you, Gabrielle. I asked you to deny that you're in love with me, but you can't do it can you? You can't deny your feelings.'

It was the flicker in her eyes before she staggered to the door that convinced Andrés he'd had the truth all along. Gabrielle was running scared.

'I never thought I would say this, Gabrielle, but you're a coward.'

Her back stiffened.

'You, the bravest person I have ever met in my life, a damned *coward*,' he snarled. 'All this time I thought it was me putting up the barriers in our relationship but they came from you too, and it's you who can't bear to let them down and see the truth. Love *terrifies* you. All these years, hiding behind your son… You only gave yourself to me because you thought I wouldn't want anything more from you than one night and now you want to throw away something that you know in your heart is beautiful and pure because you're too scared to put yourself on the line. So go on, coward, run away to your lonely bed and find something else to hide behind, but don't expect me to wait for you. I grant you your wish. Separate lives. You and I…this thing…it's over.'

Gabrielle only realised she'd left her ballet slippers behind when she found herself in the Imperium's car park barefoot. She didn't even remember getting into Andrés's elevator.

The lights that should automatically switch on at any motion within the car park stayed off. The only illumination came from what her dazed mind assumed were emergency lights because none of the exits opened.

Banging on the main doors the cars went in and out of proved futile. The duty guards, appointed to stop the public gaining access to some of the world's most expensive cars were missing.

Restless, nauseous, desperate for fresh air,

even more desperate not to think, she prowled the car park looking for another means of escape.

'I'm sorry to tell you, sir, but she seems to have vanished.'

Only moments, mere seconds, after Gabrielle left the dining room, Andrés had gathered his wits about him to give the order for her to be driven home.

'How can she just vanish?' he demanded icily.

'I don't know, sir.'

'Well don't just stand there,' he roared, furious at this time wasting. 'Go and find her.'

It was on Gabrielle's fifth circuit of the cavernous car park that her eyes finally skimmed the one car she'd been studiously avoiding.

Her feet stopped walking.

Her stare fell back on the car that had started it all.

Her eyes swam.

If this car had taken the different line, she wouldn't be standing here. The other team would have processed it. She would never have set eyes on Andrés.

The bones in her legs weakening, she pressed a hand to her swollen stomach.

If Andrés had taken the different line, the little life inside her wouldn't be there. She wouldn't be there. She would be in her apartment watching a movie she'd seen a hundred times or reading a book she'd read a dozen times. She would be thinking of going to bed soon and resting enough for her work shift.

She would be oblivious to the bliss that could be found in the arms of someone you loved.

She closed her eyes and swayed.

The elevator door pinged open.

Andrés stepped into the car park. He'd searched every inch of his apartment. The Imperium's security cameras had proved she hadn't left through the atrium. An eagle-eyed security guard had spotted the slight figure pacing the car park but a problem with the electrics, which the maintenance crew were at that moment working on, had affected the main lights and meant the figure was impossible to see clearly.

He'd known though, and he strode to the woman who'd stopped pacing and now stood motionless in front of his car.

'Are you so stubborn that you would rather stay in the dark in a locked underground car park than come back up to the apartment and leave another way?' His relief at finding her mixed with the fury still pumping through his blood at her cowardice.

Her head turned slowly to him.

Even with the minimal lighting he could see the pallor of her skin.

'Do you want to stay here all night?' he demanded.

Her throat moved.

He turned his face from her. It made his guts shred to even look at her. 'Come on,' he said tersely. 'The concierge has arranged for a car to take you home.'

After three paces he realised she still hadn't moved from her spot.

Her expression was stark. 'Do you love me?'

'If that wasn't made clear to you, then yes, I love you, and now that you've ripped out another piece of my scalp, can we get out of here?'

He set off again to the elevator.

'Andrés, I'm scared.'

Now he was the one to freeze.

'I've seen what love can do. I've lived it. I watched my mother waste away through the pain of losing my father, and Eloise...'

His heart caught in his throat. Turning slowly, he found himself caught in the dark brown eyes brimming with tears.

A wave of shame drove through him. He'd backed her into a corner and like a frightened kitten she'd come out fighting.

Rubbing her eyes, she said, 'You were wrong,

you know. It isn't love I'm frightened of. It's losing it.

'I've always been the strong one. Eloise saw it, it's why she was so insistent that I be Lucas's mother, but I never asked or wanted to be the strong one. It was a role I was given and I've never had any choice but to live up to it for everyone else's sake, and then you...'

She drew in a long breath and whispered, 'You make me feel vulnerable.' She swallowed. 'It's not something I've felt before and... Andrés, it's terrifying.'

'Enough,' he said hoarsely, his legs unlocking themselves to stride to her. Hauling her into his arms, he pressed a long kiss to the top of her head. 'Enough.'

After a moment's hesitation, Gabrielle's arms wrapped around and she held him as tightly as he held her.

He exhaled his deep relief into her sweet-smelling hair. 'No more explanations. I love you, Gabrielle. With everything I have. I fell in love with you when you were dressed as a princess and I've loved you ever since. You are everything to me and I swear that if you put your heart and your trust in me, I will never abuse it. You don't have to be the strong one any more. Just be you, because it's you I love, you with all your strength and all your vulner-abilities, and I swear I will never let you down.'

A shudder ran through Gabrielle, so power-ful she had to cling even tighter to him. When it had passed, she lifted her head to gaze up at the handsome face of the man who had stolen her heart without even trying.

Bathed in clarity, she palmed his bearded cheek.

'I love *you*,' she breathed. 'I fell in love with you when I was dressed as a princess and I've never stopped. You are everything to me, and there is nothing I want more than to marry you.'

'Ah, Gabrielle, *ma belle*,' he groaned, and then his mouth claimed hers and Gabrielle found herself bathed in the warmth of a love so deep and sincere that the last of her fears evaporated.

EPILOGUE

THE PRIEST POURED the blessed water over baby Eloise's head. To neither of her parents' surprise, she carried on sleeping, blissfully unaware of the occasion that made her the centre of attention. At eight months old, Eloise was a happy little lump who epitomised the saying of sleeping like a baby.

Once the Christening had finished, Gabrielle, Andrés, the proud godparents and the family and friends there to witness the event stepped out of the pretty church into the pretty grounds and the warm Seville sunshine.

Lucas, who'd been sat with Gabrielle's mother and brother during the service, bounded over to his parents. Having finished his first year of school, he considered himself too big to be carried any more, but, thankfully, not too big to hold his mummy and daddy's hands, and his hand was swallowed straight into Andrés's.

'Can Raul and I play football when we get home, Daddy?'

'After we've eaten.'

Everyone, the priest included, was going back to their home to continue the celebrations.

'Will you play with us?'

'Only if I can be on your team.'

Lucas turned to Gabrielle. 'Will you be goal-keeper?'

'In this dress and these shoes?' she teased. 'Ask Aunty Sophia. She was telling me only yesterday how much she loves football.'

He went running off to his favourite—and only—aunty.

Moments later, amused daggers were being thrown at Gabrielle who grinned and turned to greet Queen Catalina and her husband, Nathaniel, who'd come over to admire baby Eloise.

One day she would get used to calling her heroine a personal friend. One day.

Soon, the official photographer was calling everyone together.

Passing Eloise to Andrés, she slipped an arm around him and held Lucas's hand with the other.

'Have I told you how sexy you look in that dress?' Andrés murmured into her ear while everyone gathered and jostled around them.

She fixed him with her primmest look and slipped her hand beneath the tail of his suit jacket to pinch his bottom.

He grinned and, holding the baby firmly, kissed her.

The photographer caught the moment where their mouths pulled apart but their eyes were intimately locked together. In that picture, Lucas was beaming widely at the camera and baby Eloise's dark eyes had opened, her face a picture of contentment.

Both Gabrielle and Andrés carried a copy of it in their wallets for the rest of their lives.

* * * * *

Were you swept away by the passion of
Cinderella's One-Night Baby?
Then discover these other
Michelle Smart stories!

Pregnant Innocent Behind the Veil
Rules of Their Royal Wedding Night
Bound by the Italian's "I Do"
Christmas Baby with Her Ultra-Rich Boss
Innocent's Wedding Day with the Italian

Available now!